Very nicely he ki~~ssed~~ ~~her, even~~ if she was terribly nervous he sort of let her be nervous as he kissed her— till the pleats in her mind unfurled.

It was a kiss that had been building all night, a kiss she had wanted since introduction, and his mouth told her he had wanted the same.

'I was going to stay for one drink…' His mouth was at her ear, his body pressed into hers.

'I was actually just leaving,' she admitted as his face came back into view.

'And now look at us.'

So nice had been that kiss that he did it again.

'You smell fantastic.' She was so, so glad to be honest.

'So do you.'

'You taste fantastic,' she said. And Bridgette was the one going back for more now.

'You too.'

And he actually liked the weight of responsibility that cloaked him as he pressed her against the bonnet, his hands inching down to a silver hem. He ended their kiss and walked them back to the car. Because he wanted more for her than that—more for him than that.

Just tonight.

Carol Marinelli recently filled in a form where she was asked for her job title and was thrilled, after all these years, to be able to put down her answer as 'writer'. Then it asked what Carol did for relaxation. After chewing her pen for a moment Carol put down the truth—'writing'. The third question asked—'What are your hobbies?' Well, not wanting to look obsessed or, worse still, boring, she crossed the fingers on her free hand and answered 'swimming and tennis'. But, given that the chlorine in the pool does terrible things to her highlights, and the closest she's got to a tennis racket in the last couple of years is watching the Australian Open, I'm sure you can guess the real answer!

Recent books by Carol Marinelli:

Mills & Boon® Medical™ Romance

CORT MASON—DR DELECTABLE
HER LITTLE SECRET
ST PIRAN'S: RESCUING PREGNANT CINDERELLA—
  St Piran's Hospital
KNIGHT ON THE CHILDREN'S WARD

Mills & Boon® Modern™ Romance

AN INDECENT PROPOSITION
A SHAMEFUL CONSEQUENCE
HEART OF THE DESERT
THE DEVIL WEARS KOLOVSKY

These books are also available in eBook format from www.millsandboon.co.uk

HERS FOR
ONE NIGHT ONLY?

BY
CAROL MARINELLI

First published in Great Britain 2012
by Mills & Boon, an imprint of Harlequin (UK) Limited.
Harlequin (UK) Limited, Eton House, 18-24 Paradise Road,
Richmond, Surrey TW9 1SR

© Carol Marinelli 2012

ISBN: 978 0 263 22876 2

Harlequin (UK) policy is to use papers that are natural, renewable and recyclable products and made from wood grown in sustainable forests. The logging and manufacturing process conform to the legal environmental regulations of the country of origin.

Printed and bound in Great Britain
by CPI Antony Rowe, Chippenham, Wiltshire

If you love **Carol Marinelli**
you'll fall head over heels for her
sparkling, touching, witty debut
PUTTING ALICE BACK TOGETHER
available from MIRA® Books.

CHAPTER ONE

'YOU'RE far too available.' Bridgette didn't really know how to respond when her friend Jasmine's sympathy finally ran out. After all, she knew that Jasmine was right. 'It's me and Vince's leaving do and you won't come out *in case* your sister needs a babysitter.'

'You know it's not as simple as that,' Bridgette said.

'But it *is* as simple as that.' Jasmine was determined to stand firm this time. Her boyfriend, Vince, was a paediatric intern at the large Melbourne hospital where Bridgette had, until recently, worked, and he was heading off for a year to do relief work overseas. At what felt like the last minute the rather dizzy Jasmine had decided to join him for three months, and after a lot of paperwork and frantic applications, finally tonight there was a gathering to see them both off. 'You've put everything on hold for Courtney, you've given up a job you love so you can do agency and be more flexible—you've done everything you can to support her and look at where it's got you.'

Jasmine knew that she was being harsh, but she wanted Bridgette to cry, damn it, wanted her friend to admit the truth—that living like this was agony, that something had to give. But Bridgette refused to cry, insisting instead that she was coping—that she didn't mind doing agency work, that she loved looking after Courtney's son, Harry. 'Come out, then,' Jasmine challenged. 'If everything's as fine as you say, you deserve a night out—you haven't had one in ages. I want you there—we all want to see you. Everyone will be there…'

'What if…?' Bridgette stopped herself from saying it. She was exhausted from going over the what-ifs.

'Stop hiding behind Harry,' Jasmine said.

'I'm not.'

'Yes, you are. I know you've been hurt, but you need to put it behind you.'

And it stung, but, then, the truth often did and, yes, Bridgette conceded, maybe she was using Harry as a bit of an excuse so as not to get out there. 'Okay!' Bridgette took a deep breath and nodded. 'You're on.'

'You're coming?' Jasmine grinned.

'Looks like it.'

So instead of sitting at home, Bridgette sat in the hairdresser's and had some dark foils added to her mousey-brown hair. They made her skin look paler and her sludgy-grey eyes just a bit darker, it seemed, and with Jasmine's endless encouragement she had a wax and her nails done too and, for good measure, crammed in a little shopping.

Bridgette's bedroom was in chaos, not that Jasmine cared a bit, as they fought over mirror space and added another layer of mascara. It was a hot, humid night and already Bridgette was sweating. Her face would be shining by the time she got there at this rate, so she climbed over two laundry baskets to open her bedroom window and then attempted to find her shoes. 'I must tidy up in here.' Bridgette searched for her high-heeled sandals. Her bedroom had once been tidy—but when Harry had been born Courtney had moved in and Bridgette's two-bedroom flat had never quite recovered from housing three—actually, four at times if you counted Paul. Her love life hadn't recovered either!

Bridgette found her sandals and leant against the wall as she put them on. She surveyed the large boxes of shelves she had bought online that would hopefully help her organise things. 'I want to get these shelves put up. Dad said he'd come around and find the studs in the wall, whatever they are…'

Jasmine bit her tongue—Maurice had been saying that for months. The last thing Bridgette needed tonight was to have her parents criticised but, honestly, two more unhelpful, inflexible people you could not meet. Maurice and Betty Joyce just closed their eyes to the chaos their youngest daughter created and left it all for Bridgette to sort out.

'How do you feel?' Jasmine asked as, dressed in a guilty purchase, make-up done and high heels on, Bridgette surveyed herself in the mirror.

'Twenty-six.' Bridgette grinned at her own reflection, liking, for once, what she saw. Gone was the exhausted woman from earlier—instead she literally glowed and not with sweat either. No, it was the sheer silver dress she had bought that did the most amazing things to her rather curvy figure, and the heavenly new blusher that had wiped away the last remnants of fatigue in just a few glittery, peachy strokes.

'And single,' Jasmine nudged.

'Staying single,' Bridgette said. 'The last thing I want is a relationship.'

'Doesn't have to be a relationship,' Jasmine replied, but gave in with a small laugh. 'It does with you, though.' She looked at her friend. 'Paul was a complete bastard, you know.'

'I know.' She did not want to talk about it.

'Better to find out now than later.'

'I know that,' Bridgette snapped. She *so* did not want to talk about it—she didn't even want to think about it tonight—but thankfully Jasmine had other things on her mind.

'Ooh, I wonder if Dominic will be there. He's sex on legs, that guy...' Even though she was blissfully happy with Vince, Jasmine still raved about the paediatric locum registrar, Dominic Mansfield.

'You're just about to fly off to Africa with your boyfriend.' Bridgette grinned. 'Should you be noticing such things?'

'I can still look.' Jasmine sighed. 'Honestly, you can't help looking when Dominic's around—he's gorgeous. He just doesn't belong in our hospital. He should be on some glamorous soap or something… Anyway, I was thinking of him more for you.'

'Liar. From what you've told me about Dominic, he's not the *relationship* kind.'

'Well, he must have been at some point—he was engaged before he came to Melbourne. Mind you, he wouldn't do for you at all. He hardly speaks. He's quite arrogant really,' Jasmine mused. 'Anyway, enough about all that. Look at you.' She smiled at her friend in the mirror. 'Gorgeous, single, no commitments… You're allowed to have fun, you know.'

Except Bridgette did have commitments, even if no one could really understand them. It was those commitments that had her double-check that she had her phone in her bag. She didn't feel completely single—more she felt like a single mum with her child away on an access visit. Courtney and Harry had lived with her for a year and it had ended badly, and though she spoke little to Courtney now, she was an extremely regular babysitter.

She missed him tonight.

But, she reminded herself, he wasn't hers to miss.

Still, it was nice to be out and to catch up with everyone. They all put in some money for drinks, but unfortunately it was Jasmine who chose the wine and it was certainly a case of quantity over quality. Bridgette took a sip—she was far from a wine snob, but it really was awful and she sat on one drink all night.

'When are you coming back to us?' was the cry from her ex-colleagues.

'I'm not sure,' Bridgette responded. 'Soon, I hope.'

Yes, it was a good night; it just wasn't the same as it once had been.

She wasn't one of them any more.

She had no idea who they were talking about when they moaned about someone called Rita—how she took over in a birth, how much her voice grated. There had been a big drama last week apparently, which they were now discussing, of which Bridgette knew nothing. Slipping her phone out of her bag, she checked it, relieved to see that there were no calls, but even though she wasn't needed, even though she had nowhere else to be right now, the night was over for her.

She wasn't a midwife any more, or at best she was an occasional one—she went wherever the agency sent her. Bridgette was about to say goodbye to Jasmine, to make a discreet exit, when she was thwarted by some late arrivals, whom Jasmine marched her over to, insisting that she say hello.

'This is Rita, the new unit manager.' Jasmine introduced the two women. 'And, Rita, this is Bridgette Joyce. She used to work with us. We're trying to persuade her to come back. And this is...' He really needed no introduction, because Bridgette looked over and fell into very black eyes. The man stood apart from the rest and looked a bit out of place in the rather tacky bar, and, yes, he was as completely stunning as Jasmine had described. His black hair was worn just a little bit long and swept backwards to reveal a face that was exquisite. He was tall, slim and wearing black trousers and a fitted white shirt. He was, quite simply, divine. 'This is Dominic,' Jasmine introduced, 'our locum paediatrician.'

He didn't look like a paediatrician—oh, she knew she shouldn't label people so, but as he nodded and said hello he didn't look in the least like a man who was used to dealing with children. Jasmine was right—he should be on a soap, playing the part of a pretend doctor, or... She imagined him more a surgeon, a cosmetic surgeon perhaps, at some exclusive private practice.

'Can I get anyone a drink?' He was very smooth and polite, and there was no hint of an accent, but with such dark looks she wondered if his forebears were Italian perhaps, maybe Greek. He must have caught her staring, and when he saw that she didn't have a glass, he spoke directly to her. 'Bridgette, can I get you anything?'

'Not for me, thanks, I'm—' She was just about to say that she was leaving when Jasmine interrupted her.

'You don't need to buy a drink, Dominic. We've got loads.' Jasmine toddled over to their loud table and poured him a glass of vinegary wine and one for Bridgette too, and then handed them over. 'Come on.' Jasmine pushed, determined her friend would unwind. 'Drink up, Bridgette.'

He was terribly polite because he accepted it graciously and took a sip of the drink and managed not to wince. But as Bridgette took a tiny sip, she did catch his eye, and there was a hint of a shared smile, if it could even be called that.

'It's good that you could make it, Dominic.' Vince

came over. He had just today finished his paediatric rotation, and Bridgette had worked with him on Maternity for a while before she'd left. 'I know that it hasn't been a great day.'

She watched as Dominic gave a brief nod, gave practically nothing back to that line of conversation—instead, he changed the subject. 'So,' he asked, 'when do you fly?'

'Monday night,' Vince said, and spoke a little about the project he was joining.

'Well,' said Dominic, 'all the best with it.'

He really didn't waste words, did he? Bridgette thought as Jasmine polished her cupid's bow and happily took Vince's hand and wandered off, leaving Bridgette alone with him and trying not to show just how awkward she felt.

'Careful,' she said as his glass moved to his lips. 'Remember how bad it tastes.'

She was rewarded with the glimpse of a smile.

'Do you want me to get you something else?'

Yikes, she hadn't been fishing for drinks. 'No, no...' Bridgette shook her head. 'Jasmine would be offended. I'm fine. I was just...' Joking, she didn't add, trying to make conversation. Gorgeous he might be to look at but he really didn't say very much. 'You're at the hospital, then?' Bridgette asked.

'Just as a fill-in,' Dominic said. 'I've got a consultant's position starting in a couple of weeks in Sydney.' He named a rather impressive hospital and that just about summed him up, Bridgette decided—rather impressive and very, very temporary.

'Your family is there?'

'That's right,' he said, but didn't elaborate. 'You work on Maternity?' Dominic frowned, because he couldn't place her.

'I used to,' Bridgette explained. 'I left six months ago. I've been doing agency…'

'Why?'

It was a very direct question, one she wasn't quite expecting, one she wasn't really sure how to answer.

'The hours are more flexible,' she said, 'the money's better…' And it was the truth, but only a shred of it, because she missed her old job very badly. She'd just been accepted as a clinical nurse specialist when she'd left. She adored everything about midwifery, and now she went wherever the agency sent her. As she was qualified as a general nurse, she could find herself in nursing homes, on spinal units, sometimes in psych. She just worked and got on with it, but she missed doing what she loved the most.

He really didn't need to hear it, so back on went the smile she'd been wearing all night. 'And it means that I get to go out on a Saturday night.' The moment she said them, she wanted those words back, wished she could retrieve them. She knew that she sounded like some sort of party girl, especially with what came next.

'I can see it has benefits,' Dominic said, and she swore he glanced down at the hand that was holding the glass, and for a dizzy moment she realised she was being appraised. 'If you have a young family.'

'Er, no.' Oh, help, she *was* being appraised. He was looking at her, the same way she might look at shoes in a window and tick off her mental list of preferences— too flat, too high, nice colour, shame about the bow. Wrong girl, she wanted to say to him, I'm lace-up-shoe boring.

'You don't have children?'

'No,' she said, and something twisted inside, because if she told him about Harry she would surely burst into tears. She could just imagine Dominic's gorgeous face sort of sliding into horrified boredom if the newly foiled, for once groomed woman beside him told him she felt as if her guts were being torn, that right now, right this very minute, she was having great difficulty not pulling out her phone to check if there had been a text or a call from Courtney. Right now she wanted to drive past where her sister was living with her friend Louise and make sure that there wasn't a wild party raging. She scrambled for something to say, anything to say, and of course she again said the wrong thing.

'Sorry that you had a bad day.' She watched his jaw tighten a fraction, knew, given his job, that it was a stupid thing to say, especially when her words tumbled out in a bright and breezy voice. But the false smile she had plastered on all night seemed to be infusing her brain somehow, she was so incredibly out of practice with anything remotely social.

He gave her the same brief nod that he had given Vince, then a very brief smile and very smoothly excused himself.

'Told you!' Jasmine was over in a flash the minute he was gone. 'Oh, my God, you were talking for ages.'

'For two minutes.'

'That's ages for him!' Jasmine breathed. 'He hardly says a word to anyone.'

'Jasmine!' She rolled her eyes at her friend. 'You can stop this very moment.' Bridgette let out a small gurgle of laughter. 'I think I've just been assessed as to my suitability for a one-nighter. Honestly, he's shameless… He asked if I had children and everything. Maybe he's worried I've got stretch marks and a baggy vagina.'

It was midwife-speak, and as she made Jasmine laugh, she laughed herself. The two women really laughed for the first time in a long, long time, and it was so good for Bridgette to be with her friend before she jetted off, because Jasmine had helped her through this difficult time. She didn't want to be a misery at her friends' leaving do, so she kept up the conversation a little. They giggled about lithe, toned bodies and the temptresses who would surely writhe on his white rug in his undoubtedly immaculate city apartment. It *was* a white rug, they decided, laughing, for a man like Dominic was surely far too tasteful for animal prints. And he'd make you a cocktail on arrival, for this was the first-class lounge of one-night stands, and on and on they went… Yes, it was so good to laugh.

* * *

Dominic could hear her laughter as he spoke with a colleague, as again he was offered yet more supposed consolation for a 'bad day'. He wished that people would just say nothing, wished he could simply forget.

It had been a… He searched for the expletive to best describe his day, chose it, but knew if he voiced it he might just be asked to leave, which wouldn't be so bad, but, no, he took a mouthful of vinegar and grimaced as it met the acid in his stomach.

He hated his job.

Was great at it.

Hated it.

Loved it.

Did it.

He played ping-pong in his mind with a ball that broke with every hit.

He wanted that hard ball tonight, one that bounced back on every smash, one that didn't crumple if you hammered it.

He wanted to be the doctor who offered better answers.

Today he had seen the dominos falling, had scrambled to stop them, had done everything to reset them, but still they'd fallen—click, click, click—racing faster than he could halt them till he'd known absolutely what was coming and had loathed that he'd been the only one who could see it.

'Where there's life there's hope' had been offered several times.

Actually, no, he wanted to say as he'd stared at another batch of blood results and read off the poisons that had filled this tiny body.

'There is hope, though...' the parents had begged, and he had refused to flinch at the frantic eyes that had scanned his face as he'd delivered news.

He loved hope, he craved hope and had searched so hard for it today, but he also knew when hope was gone, said it before others would. Unlike others, he faced the inevitable—because it was either cardiac massage and all lights blazing, or a cuddle without the tubes at the end.

Yes, it came down to that.

Yes, it had been a XXXX of a day.

He had sat with the parents till ten p.m. and then entered a bar that was too bright, stood with company that was too loud and tasted wine that could dissolve an olive, and hated that he missed her. How could you miss a woman you didn't even like? He hated that she'd ring tonight and that he might be tempted to go back. That in two weeks' time he'd see her. Shouldn't he be over Arabella by now? Maybe it was just because he had had a 'bad day'. Not that he and Arabella had ever really spoken about work—oh, they'd discussed their career paths of course, but never the day-to-day details. They'd never talked about days such as this, Dominic mused.

Then he had seen her—Bridgette. In a silver dress and with a very wide smile, with gorgeous nails and polished hair, she had drawn his eye. Yet on inspection there was more behind that polished façade than he cared to explore, more than he needed tonight.

He *had* been checking for a wedding ring.

What no one understood was that he preferred to find one.

Married women were less complicated, knew the rules from the start, for they had so much more to lose than he did.

Bridgette was complicated.

He'd read her, because he read women well. He could see the hurt behind those grey eyes, could see the effort that went into her bright smile. She was complicated and he didn't need it. But, on the way down to her ring finger, he'd noticed very pale skin and a tapestry of freckles, and he'd wondered where the freckles stopped, had wondered far too many things.

He didn't need an ounce of emotion tonight, not one more piece, which was why he had excused himself and walked away. But perhaps he'd left gut instinct in his car tonight, the radar warning that had told him to keep his distance dimmed a fraction as he looked over to where she stood, laughing with her friend.

'Hey, Dominic…' He heard a low, seductive voice and turned to the pretty blonde who stood before him, a nurse who worked in Theatre and one whose husband seemed to be perpetually away. 'So brilliant to see you tonight.' He looked into eyes that were blue and glittered with open invitation, saw the ring on her finger and the spray tan on her arm on the way down. 'I just finished a late shift. Wasn't sure I'd make it.'

'Are you on tomorrow?' someone asked.

'No,' she answered. 'And I've got the weekend to my-self. Geoff's away.' Her eyes flicked to his and Dominic met her gaze, went to take another sip of his drink and then, remembering how it tasted, changed his mind, and he changed his mind about something else too—he couldn't stomach the taste of fake tan tonight.

Then he heard Bridgette laughing, looked over and ignored his inner radar, managed to convince himself that he had read her wrong.

He knew now what Bridgette's middle name was.

Escape.

'People are talking about going for something to eat…' Vince came over and snaked his arm around Jasmine, and they shared a kiss as Bridgette stood, pretending not to feel awkward—actually, not so awkward now that she and Jasmine had had such a laugh. She wasn't going out to dinner, or to a club, but at least she and Jasmine had had some fun—but then the waitress came over and handed her a glass.

'For me?' Bridgette frowned.

'He said to be discreet.' The waitress nodded her head in Dominic's direction. 'I'll get rid of your other glass.'

Double yikes!

She glanced over to black eyes that were waiting to meet hers.

Wrong girl, she wanted to semaphore back—so very, very wrong for you, Dominic, she wanted to signal. It took me weeks to have sex with Paul, I mean weeks, and you're only here for two. And I don't think I'm very good at it anyway. At least he hinted at that when we broke up. But Bridgette didn't have any flags handy and wouldn't know what to do if she had them anyway, so she couldn't spell it out; she only had her eyes and they held his.

She lifted the glass of temptation he offered and the wine slipped onto her tongue and down her throat. It tasted delicious—cold and expensive and not at all what she was used to.

She felt her cheeks burn as she dragged her eyes from him and back to her friend and tried to focus on what Jasmine was saying—something about Mexican, and a night that would never end. She sipped her champagne that was far too nice, far too moreish, and Bridgette knew she had to get out of there. 'Not for me,' she said to Jasmine, feeling the scald of his eyes on her shoulder as she spoke. 'Honestly, Jasmine…' She didn't need to make excuses with her friend.

'I know.' Jasmine smiled. 'It really is great that you came out.'

It had been. Bridgette was relieved that she'd made it this far for her friend and also rather relieved to escape from the very suave Dominic—he was so out of her league and she also knew they were flirting. Dominic had the completely wrong impression of her—he thought she worked agency for the money and flexibility, so that she could choose her shifts at whim and party hard on a Saturday night.

If only he knew the truth.

Still, he was terribly nice.

Not nice, she corrected. Not *nice* nice, more toe-curlingly sexy and a dangerous nice. Still, no one was leaving. Instead he had made his way over, the music seemed to thud low in her stomach and for a bizarre moment as he joined them she thought he was about to lean over and kiss her.

Just like that, in front of everyone.

And just like that, in front of everyone, she had the ridiculous feeling that she'd comply.

It was safer to leave, to thank him for the drink, to say she wasn't hungry, to hitch up her bag and get the hell out of there, to ignore the dangerous dance in her mind.

'I'll see you on Monday,' she said to Jasmine.

'You can help me pack!'

The group sort of moved out of the bar as she did and walked towards the Mexican restaurant. There had been a burst of summer rain but it hadn't cleared the air. Instead it was muggy, the damp night air clinging to her cheeks, to her legs and arms as her eyes scanned the street for a taxi.

'Are you sure you don't want something to eat?' Dominic asked.

And she should say no—she really should walk away now, Bridgette told herself. She didn't even like Mexican food, but he was gorgeous and it had been ages since there had been even a hint of a flirt. And she was twenty-six and maybe just a bit flattered that someone as sophisticated as he was was paying her attention. Her wounded ego could certainly use the massage and she'd just checked her phone and things seemed fine, so Bridgette took a deep breath and forced back that smile.

'Sounds great.'

'Good,' he replied, except she was confused, because he then said goodbye to Vince and Jasmine as Bridgette stood on the pavement, blinking as the group all bundled into a restaurant and just the two of them remained. Then he turned and smiled. 'Let's get something to eat, then.'

'I thought…' She didn't finish her sentence, because he aimed his keys at a car, a very nice car, which lit up in response, and she glanced at her phone again and there wasn't a single message.

Her chariot awaited.

She climbed in the car and sank into the leather and held her breath as Dominic walked around to the driver's side.

She didn't do things like this.

Ever.

But there was a part of her that didn't want to say goodnight.

A part of her that didn't want to go back to an empty flat and worry about Harry.

They drove though the city; he blasted on the air-conditioner and it was bliss to feel the cool air on her cheeks. They drove in silence until his phone rang and she glanced to the dashboard where it sat in its little charger and the name 'Arabella' flashed up on his screen. Instead of making an excuse, he turned for a brief second and rolled his eyes. 'Here we go.'

'Sorry?'

'The maudlin Saturday night phone call,' Dominic said, grinding the gears. 'How much she misses me, how she didn't mean it like that...'

The phone went black.

'Your ex?'

'Yep.' He glanced over to her. 'You can answer it if she rings again.' He flashed her a smile, a devilish smile that had her stomach flip. 'Tell her we're in bed—that might just silence her.'

'Er, no!' She grinned. 'I don't do things like that.'

On both counts.

'Were you serious?' she asked, because she couldn't really imagine him serious about anyone. Mind you, Jasmine had said they'd been engaged.

'Engaged,' he said. 'For a whole four weeks.'

And he pulled his foot back from the accelerator because he realised he was driving too fast, but he hated the phone calls, hated that sometimes he was tempted to answer, to slip back into life as he once had known it.

And end up like his parents, Dominic reminded himself.

He'd lived through their hellish divorce as a teenager, had seen their perfect life crumble, and had no intention of emulating it. With Arabella he had taken his time. They had been together for two years and he thought he had chosen well—gorgeous, career-minded and she didn't want children. In fact, it had turned out, she didn't want anything that was less than perfect.

'You're driving too fast.' Her voice broke into his thoughts. 'I don't make a very good passenger.' She smiled. 'I think I'm a bit of a control freak.'

He slowed down, the car swishing through the damp city streets, and then they turned into the Arts Centre car park. Walking through it, she could hear her heels ringing on the cement, and even though it was her town, it was Dominic who knew where he was going—it had been ages since she had been in the heart of the city. She didn't feel out of place in her silver dress. The theatres were spilling out and there were people everywhere dressed to the nines and heading for a late dinner.

She found herself by a river—looking out on it from behind glass. She was at a table, with candles and silver and huge purple menus and a man she was quite sure she couldn't handle. He'd been joking in the car about telling his ex they were in bed, she knew it, but not really—she knew that too.

'What do you want to eat?'

Bridgette wasn't that hungry—she felt a little bit sick, in fact—but she looked through the menu and tried to make up her mind.

'I…' She didn't have the energy to sit through a meal. Really, she ought to tell him now, that the night would not be ending as he was undoubtedly expecting. 'I'm not very hungry…'

'We can get dessert and coffee if you want.'

'I wouldn't mind the cheese platter.'

'Start at the end.' He gave her a smile and placed the order—water for him and cognac for her, he suggested, and, heaven help her, the waiter asked if she wanted it warmed.

'Dominic...' She took a deep breath as their platter arrived, a gorgeous platter of rich cheeses and fruits. 'I think—'

'I think we just ought to enjoy,' he interrupted.

'No.' Bridgette gulped. 'I mean...' She watched as he smeared cheese on a cracker and offered it to her.

'I don't like blue cheese.'

'Then you haven't had a good one.'

He wasn't wrong there!

He took a bite instead and her hand shook as she reached for the knife, tasted something she was quite sure she didn't like and found out it was, in fact, amazing.

'Told you.'

'You did.' She looked at the platter, at the grapes and dates, like some lush oil painting, and she knew the dance that was being played and the flirting and the seduction that was to come, and it terrified her. 'I don't think I should be here...' She scrabbled in her bag, would pay the bill, knew that she must end this.

'Bridgette.' He wasn't a bastard—he really wasn't. Yes, he'd been playing the field since his engagement had ended, and, yes, he had every intention of continuing to do so, but he only played with those who were happy with the rules, and he knew now for sure that she wasn't. 'It's cheese.'

She lifted troubled eyes to his.

'No, it isn't—it's the ride home after.'

He liked her. He hadn't wanted emotion tonight, and yet she made him smile as a tear washed away the last of her foundation and he could see freckles on her nose. 'Bridgette, it's cheese and conversation.' He took her hand, and she started to tell him he didn't want just cheese and conversation, oh, no, she knew it very well. She told him she wasn't the girl in the silver dress who partied and he held her hand as she babbled about zebra-print rugs, no white ones, and cocktails. 'Bridgette.' He was incredibly close to adoring her, to leaning over and kissing her right now. 'It's cheese and conversation and then I'll take you home.' He looked at her mouth and he was honest. 'Maybe just one kiss goodnight.'

Oh, but she wanted her kiss.

Just one.

'That leads nowhere,' she said.

'That leads nowhere,' he assured her.

'We're not suited,' she said, and was incredibly grateful that he nodded.

'We're completely incompatible,' Dominic agreed.

'And I'm sorry if I've misled you…'

'You didn't.' He was very magnanimous, smearing more cheese and this time handing it to her, no, wait, feeding her, and it wasn't so much seductive as nice. 'I *let* myself be misled,' he said, and he handed her her cognac. 'I knew from the start you were nice.' He gave her a smile. 'And you are, Bridgette.'

'So are you.'

'Oh, no,' he assured her. 'I'm not.'

CHAPTER TWO

IT FELT so good to feel so good and it was as if they both knew that they didn't have long. It was terribly hard to explain it, but now that there wasn't sex on the menu, now they'd cleared that out of the way, they could relax and just be.

For a little while.

She took a sip of cognac and it burnt all the way down, a delicious burn.

'Nice?' Dominic asked.

'Too nice,' she admitted.

And he hadn't wanted conversation, or emotion, but he was laughing, talking, sharing, and that XXXX of a day melted away with her smile.

So they worked the menu backwards and ordered dessert, chocolate soufflé for Bridgette and watermelon and mint sorbet for him. As he sampled his dish, Bridgette wanted a taste—not a spoonful, more a taste of his cool, watermelon-and-mint-flavoured tongue— and she flushed a little as he offered her the spoon. 'Want some?' Dominic said.

She shook her head, asked instead about his work,

and he told her a bit about his plans for his career, and she told him about the lack of plans for hers.

'You love midwifery, though?' Dominic checked.

'I am hoping to go back to it.' Bridgette nodded. 'It's just been a bit of a complicated year...' She didn't elaborate and she was glad that he didn't push. Yes, she loved midwifery, she answered, loved babies.

'You want your own?' He asked the same question that everyone did when they heard her job.

'One day maybe...' Bridgette gave a vague shrug. Had he asked a couple of years ago she'd have told him that she wanted millions, couldn't wait to have babies of her own. Only now she simply couldn't see it. She couldn't imagine a place or a time where it might happen, couldn't imagine really trusting a man again. She didn't tell him that of course—that wasn't what tonight was about. Instead she gave a vague nod. 'I think so. You?' she asked, and he admitted that he shuddered at the very thought.

'You're a paediatrician.' Bridgette laughed.

'Doesn't mean I have to want my own. Anyway,' he added, 'I know what can go wrong.' He shook his head and was very definite. 'Nope, not for me.' He told her that he had a brother, Chris, when Bridgette said she had a sister, Courtney. Neither mentioned Arabella or Paul, and Bridgette certainly didn't mention Harry.

Tonight it was just about them.

And then they ordered coffee and talked some more.

And then another coffee.

And the waiters yawned, and Dominic and Bridgette

looked around the restaurant and realised it was just the two of them left.

And it was over too soon, Bridgette thought as he paid the bill and they left. It was as if they were trying to cram so much into one night; almost as if it was understood that this really should deserve longer. It was like a plane trip alongside a wonderful companion: you knew you would be friends, more than friends perhaps, if you had more time, but you were both heading off to different lives. He to further his career and then back to his life in Sydney,

She to, no doubt, more of the same.

Except they had these few hours together and neither wanted them to end.

They walked along the river and to the bridge, leant over it and looked into the water, and still they spoke, about silly things, about music and videos and movies they had watched or that they thought the other really should see. He was nothing like the man she had assumed he was when they had been introduced in the bar—he was insightful and funny and amazing company. In fact, nothing at all like the remote, aloof man that Jasmine had described.

And she was nothing like he'd expected either when they had been introduced. Dominic was very careful about the women he dated in Melbourne; he had no interest in settling down, not even for a few weeks. Occasionally he got it wrong, and it would end in tears a few days later. Not his of course—it was always the women who wanted more than he was prepared to give, and Dominic had decided he was never giving that part of himself again. But there was a strange regret in the air as he drove her home—a rare regret for Dominic—because here was a woman he actually wouldn't mind getting to know a little more, one who might get him over those last stubborn, lingering remnants of Arabella.

He'd been joking about Bridgette answering the phone.

Sort of.

Actually, it wasn't such a bad idea. He couldn't face going back to Sydney while there was still weakness, didn't want to slip back into the picture-perfect life that had been prescribed to him since birth.

And it was strange because had they met at the start of his stay here, he was sure, quite sure, time would have moved more slowly. Now, though, it seemed that the beach road that led to her home, a road he was quite positive usually took a good fifteen minutes, seemed to be almost over in eight minutes and still they were talking, still they were laughing, as the car gobbled up their time.

'You should watch it.' She was talking about something on the internet, something she had found incredibly funny. 'Tonight when you get in.' She glanced at the clock on the dashboard and saw that it was almost two. 'I mean, this morning.'

'You watch it too.' He grinned. 'We can watch simultaneously...' His fingers tightened on the wheel and he ordered his mind not to voice the sudden direction it had taken—thankfully those thoughts went unsaid and unheard.

'I can't get on the internet,' Bridgette grumbled, trying desperately not to think similar thoughts. 'I've got a virus.' She swung her face to him. 'My computer, I mean, not...' What was wrong with her mouth? Bridgette thought as she turned her burning face to look out of the window. Why did everything lead to sex with him? 'Anyway,' she said, 'you should watch it.'

There was a roundabout coming up, the last roundabout, Bridgette knew, before her home, and it felt like her last chance at crazy, their last chance. And, yes, it was two a.m., but it could have been two p.m.; it was just a day that was running out and they wanted to chase it. She stole a look over at his delectable profile and to the olive hands that gripped the steering-wheel—it would be like leaving the cinema in the middle of the best movie ever without a hope of finding out the end. And she wanted more detail, wanted to know how it felt to be made love to by a man like him. She'd been truthful when she'd spoken to Jasmine—a relationship was the very last thing that she wanted now. Maybe this way had merit... '*We* should watch it.'

'Your computer's not working,' he pointed out.

'Yours is.' The flick of the indicator signalling right was about half the speed of her heart.

'Bridgette...' He wasn't a bastard—he was incredibly, incredibly nice, because they went three times round the roundabout as he made very sure.

'I don't want you to regret…' He was completely honest. 'I leave in two weeks.'

'I won't regret it.' She'd firmly decided that she wouldn't. 'After much consideration I have decided I would very much regret it if I didn't.' She gave him a smile. 'I want my night.'

She did. And he was lovely, because he did not gun the car home. It was so much nicer than she would ever be able to properly remember, but she knew for many nights she would try.

She wanted to be able to hold on to the moment when he turned and told her that he couldn't wait till they got all the way back to the city for the one kiss they had previously agreed to. She wanted to remember how they stopped at a lookout, gazed out at the bay, leant against his bonnet and watched the glittering view, and it felt as if time was suspended. She wanted to bottle it somehow, because she wasn't angry with Courtney at that moment, or worried for Harry. For the first time in ages she had a tiny glimpse of calm, of peace, a moment where she felt all was well.

Well, not calm, but it was a different sort of stress from the one she was used to as he moved his face to hers. Very nicely he kissed her, even if she was terribly nervous. He let her be nervous as he kissed her— till the pleats in her mind unfurled. It was a kiss that had been building all night, a kiss she had wanted since their introduction, and his mouth told her he had wanted the same.

'I was going to stay for one drink…' His mouth was at her ear, his body pressed into hers.

'I was just leaving,' she admitted as his face came back to view.

'And now look at us.'

So nice was that kiss that he did it again.

'You smell fantastic.' She was glad, to be honest, to have only him on her mind. He smelt as expensive as he looked and he tasted divine. She would never take this dress to the dry cleaner's, she thought as his scent wrapped around them, and his mouth was at her neck and under her hair. He was dragging in the last breaths of the perfume she had squirted on before going out and soaking in the scent of the salon's rich shampoo and the warm fragrance of woman.

'So do you,' he said.

'You taste fantastic,' Bridgette said. She was the one going back for more now.

'You too.'

And he liked the weight of responsibility that cloaked him as he pressed her against the bonnet and his hands inched down to a silver hem. He could feel her soft thighs and wanted to lift her dress, but he wanted to know if her legs too were freckled, so he ended the kiss. He wanted more for her than that, more for himself than that.

Just tonight, Dominic assured himself as she did the same.

'What?' He caught her looking at him as they headed for his home, and grinned.

'Nothing.' She smiled back.

'Go on, say what you're thinking.'

'Okay.' So she did. 'You don't look like a paediatrician.'

'What is a paediatrician supposed to look like?'

'I don't know,' Bridgette admitted. 'Okay, you don't *seem* like a paediatrician.' She couldn't really explain it, but he laughed.

They laughed.

And when she told him that she imagined him more a cosmetic surgeon, with some exclusive private practice, his laugh turned wry. 'You're mistaking me for my father.'

'I don't think so,' Bridgette said.

And he pulled her towards him, because it was easier than thinking, easier than admitting he wasn't so sure of her verdict, that lately he seemed to be turning more and more into his father, the man he respected least.

It was three o'clock and she felt as if they were both trying to escape morning.

There wasn't a frantic kiss through the front door—instead the energy that swirled was more patient.

It was a gorgeous energy that waited as he made her coffee and she went to the bathroom and he had the computer on when she returned. They did actually watch it together.

'I showed this to Jasmine—' there were tears rolling down her face, but from laughter '—and she didn't think it was funny.'

And he was laughing too, more than he ever had. He

hadn't had a night like this in ages—in fact, he couldn't recall one ever.

Okay, she would try to remember the details, how he didn't cringe when she pretended his desk was a piano; instead he sang.

It was the most complicated thing to explain—that she could sing to him, that, worse, he could take the mug that was the microphone and do the same to her!

'We should be ashamed of ourselves.' She admired their reflection in the computer as they took a photo.

'Very ashamed,' he agreed.

She thought he was like this, Dominic realised, that this was how his usual one-night stands went. Didn't she understand that this was as rare for him as it was for her? He hadn't been like this even with Arabella.

He didn't just want anyone tonight; he wanted her.

It was an acute want that tired now of being patient and so too did hers. As their mouths met on time and together, he kissed her to the back of the sofa. It felt so seamless, so right, because not for a second did Bridgette think, Now he's going to kiss me. One moment they were laughing and the next they were kissing. It was a transition that was as simple as that.

It was his mouth and his taste and the slide of his tongue.

It was her mouth and a kiss that didn't taste of plastic, that tasted of her tongue, and he kissed her and she curled into it. She loved the feel of his mouth and the roam of his hands and the way her body was craving his—it was a kiss that was potent, everything a kiss could be, distilled into one delicious dose.

He took off her dress, because he wanted to see *her*, not the woman in silver, and his eyes roamed. They roamed as he took off her bra and he answered his earlier question because her freckles stopped only where her bikini would be. There were two unfreckled triangles that wanted his mouth, but he talked to her as well and what she didn't know was how rare that was.

He left control behind and was out of his mind.

He wanted her in France, he told her as he licked her nipple.

Topless and naked on the beach beside him, and new freckles on her breasts. She closed her eyes and she could smell the sun oil, could feel the heat from the sun that shone in France and the coolness of his tongue on sunburnt nipples. He pressed her into the couch and she pressed back to him.

She was lying down and could feel him hard against her and she didn't think twice, just slid his zipper down.

She could hear her own moan as she held him and he lifted his head.

'We're not going to make it to the bedroom, are we?'

'Not a hope,' she admitted.

Was this what it was like?

To be free.

To be irresponsible.

More, please, she wanted to sob, because she wanted to live on the edge for ever, never wanted this night to end.

She wanted this man who took off his trousers and

kept condoms in his wallet, and it didn't offend her—
she already knew what he was like, after all.

'Bastard.' She grinned.

And he knew her too.

'Sorry,' he said. In their own language he apologised
for the cad that he was and told her that he wasn't being
one tonight.

This was different.

So different that he sat her up.

Sank to his knees on the edge of the sofa.

And pulled her bottom towards him.

'Let's get rid of these.' He was shameless. He dis-
pensed with anything awkward, just slid her panties
down, and she did remember staring up at the ceiling as
his tongue slid up a pale, freckled thigh that didn't taste
of fake tan and then he dived right in. As he licked and
teased and tasted she would remember for ever thinking, Is this me?

And she was grateful for his experience, for his skill,
for the mastery of his tongue, because it was a whole
new world and tonight she got to step into it.

'Relax,' he said, when she forgot to for a moment.

So she did, just closed her eyes and gave in to it.

'Where's the rug?' she asked as he slid her to the
floor.

'No rug,' he said.

He maybe should get one, was her last semi-coherent
thought, because the carpet burnt in her back as he moved
inside her, a lovely burn, and then it was his turn to sam-

ple the carpet for he toppled her over, still deep inside her, and she was on top.

Don't look down.

It wasn't even a semi-coherent thought; it was more a familiar warning that echoed in her head.

Don't look down—but she did, she looked down from the tightrope that recently she'd been walking.

She glimpsed black eyes that were open as she closed hers and came, and he watched her expression, felt her abandon, and then his eyes closed as he came too. Yes, feeling those last bucks deep inside her she looked down and it didn't daunt her, didn't terrify. It exhilarated her as greedily he pulled her head down and kissed her.

'It's morning,' he said as they moved to the bedroom, the first sunlight starting.

Better still as she closed her eyes to the new day, there was no regret.

CHAPTER THREE

IT WAS like waking up to an adult Christmas.

The perfect morning, Bridgette thought as she stretched out in the wrinkled bed.

She must have slept through the alarm on her phone and he must have got up, for there was the smell of coffee in the air. If she thought there might be a little bit of embarrassment, that they both might be feeling a touch awkward this morning, she was wrong.

'Morning.' Dominic was delighted by her company, which was rare for him. He had the best job in the world to deal with situations such as this—in fact, since in Melbourne, he had a permanent alarm call set for eight a.m. at weekends. He would answer the phone to the recorded message, talk for a brief moment, and then hang up and apologise to the woman in his bed. He would explain that something had come up at work and that he had no choice but to go in.

It was a back-up plan that he often used, but he didn't want to use it today. Today he'd woken up before his alarm call and had headed out to the kitchen, made two coffees and remembered from last night that she took sugar. He thought about breakfast in bed and perhaps another walk to the river, to share it in daylight this time. Sunday stretched out before him like a long, luxurious yawn, a gorgeous pause in his busy schedule.

'What time is it?' Bridgette yawned too.

'Almost eight.' He climbed back into bed and he was delicious. 'I was thinking...' He looked down at where she lay. 'Do you want to go out somewhere nice for breakfast?'

'In a silver dress?' Bridgette grinned. 'And high heels?'

'Okay,' he said. 'Then I guess we've no option but to spend the day in bed.' She reached for her coffee and, as she always did when Harry wasn't with her, she reached for her phone to check for messages. Then she saw that it wasn't turned on and a knot of dread tightened in her stomach as she pressed the button.

'Is everything okay?'

'Sure.' Only it wasn't. She hadn't charged her phone yesterday; with Jasmine arriving and going out she hadn't thought to plug it in. Her phone could have been off for hours—anything could have happened and she wouldn't even know. She took a sip of her coffee and tried to calm herself down. Told herself she was being ridiculous, that she had to stop worrying herself sick, but it wasn't quite so easy and after a moment she turned and forced a smile. 'As much as I'd love to spend the day in bed, I really am going to have to get home.'

'Everything okay?' He checked again, because he could sense the change in her. One moment ago she'd been yawning and stretching; now she was as jumpy as a cat.

'Of course,' Bridgette said. 'I've just got a lot on...'

She saw the flash of confusion in his eyes and it could have irritated her—in fact, she wanted it to irritate her. After all, why shouldn't she have a busy day planned? Why should he just assume that she'd want a day with him? But that didn't work, because somehow last night had not been as casual as she was now making it out to be. It needed to be, Bridgette reminded herself as she turned away from his black eyes—she felt far safer with their one-night rule, far safer not trusting him. 'I'll get a taxi,' she said as she climbed out of bed and found her crumpled dress and then realised she'd have to go through the apartment to locate her underwear.

'Don't be ridiculous—I'll drive you home,' Dominic said, and he lay there as she padded out. He could hear her as she pulled on her panties and bra, and he tried not to think about last night and the wonderful time they'd had. Not just the sex, but before that, lying on the sofa watching clips on the computer, or the car ride home.

It wasn't usually him getting sentimental. Normally it was entirely the other way round.

'You really don't have to give me a lift.' She stood at the door, dressed now and holding her shoes in her hand, last night's mascara smudged beneath her eyes, her hair wild and curly, and he wanted her back in his bed. 'It's no problem to get a taxi.'

'I'll get my keys.'

And she averted her eyes as he climbed out of the bed, as he did the same walk as her and located his clothes all crumpled on the floor. She wished the balloon would pop and he'd look awful all messed and unshaven. She could smell them in the room and the computer was still on and their photo was there on the screen and *how* they'd been smiling.

'Bridgette...' He so wasn't used to this. 'You haven't even had your coffee.'

'I really do need to get back.'

'Sure.'

And talking was incredibly awkward, especially at the roundabout.

She wanted the indicator on, wanted him to turn the car around and take them back to bed, and, yes, she could maybe tell him about Harry.

About Courtney.

About the whole sorry mess.

End the dream badly.

After all, he was only here for two weeks, and even if he hadn't been, she could hardly expect someone as glamorous and gorgeous as him to understand.

She didn't want him to understand, she didn't want him to know, so instead she blew out a breath and let the sat nav lead him to her door.

'Good luck in Sydney.' She really was terrible at this one-night thing.

'Bridgette.' He had broken so many rules for her and he did it again. 'I know that you're busy today, but maybe...'

'Hey!' She forced a smile, dragged it up from her guts and slathered it on her face and turned to him. 'We're not suited, remember?'

'Completely incompatible.' He forced a smile too.

He gave her a kiss but could sense her distraction.

She climbed out of the car and she didn't say good-bye because she couldn't bear to, didn't turn around because she knew she'd head back to his arms, to his car, to escape.

But she couldn't escape the niggle in her stomach that told her things were less than fine and it niggled louder as she made a half-hearted attempt at cleaning her room. By midday her answer came.

'Can you have Harry tonight?'

'I can't,' Bridgette said. 'I'm on an early shift in the morning...' Then she closed her eyes. She had reported her sister a couple of months ago to social services and finally voiced her concerns. Oh, there was nothing spe-cific, but she could not simply stand by and do nothing. Since she'd asked Courtney to leave her flat, things had become increasingly chaotic and in the end she'd felt she had no choice but to speak out. Not to Jasmine or her friends—she didn't want to burden them. Instead she had spoken to people who might help. Her concerns had been taken seriously, and anger had ripped through her family that she could do such a thing. Sour grapes, Courtney had called it, because of what had happened between her and Paul. And then Courtney had admit-ted that, yes, she did like to party, she was only eighteen, after all, but never when Harry was around. She always made sure that Harry was taken care of.

By Bridgette.

And as she stood holding the phone, Bridgette didn't want to find out what might happen if she didn't say yes.

'I'll ring the agency,' Bridgette said. 'See if I can change to a late shift.'

Even if it was awkward talking to her sister when she dropped him off, Bridgette really was delighted to see Harry. At eighteen months he grew more gorgeous each day. His long blond curls fell in ringlets now and he had huge grey eyes like his aunt's.

Courtney had been a late baby for Maurice and Betty. Bridgette delivered babies to many so-called older women, but it was as if her parents had been old for ever—and they had struggled with the wilful Courtney from day one. It had been Bridgette who had practically brought her up, dealing with the angst and the crises that always seemed to surround Courtney, as her parents happily tuned out and carried on with their routines.

It had been Bridgette who had told them that their sixteen-year-old daughter was pregnant, Bridgette who had held Courtney's hand in the delivery room, Bridgette who had breathed with hope when Courtney, besotted with her new baby, had told Harry that she'd always be there for him.

'And I'll always be there for you,' Bridgette had said to her sister.

And Courtney was taking full advantage of that.

By seven, when Harry had had supper and been bathed, dressed in mint-green pyjamas, one of the many pairs Bridgette kept for him, and she had patted him off to sleep, she heard a car pulling up outside. She heard an expensive engine turning off, and then the sound of shoes on the steps outside her ground-floor flat, and she knew that it was him, even before she peeked through the blinds.

There was a loud ring of the bell and the noise made Harry cry.

And as Dominic stood on the step, there was his answer as to why she'd had to dash off that morning.

He waited a suitable moment, and Bridgette waited a moment too, rubbing Harry's back, telling him to go back to sleep, ignoring the bell. They were both quietly relieved when she didn't answer the door.

Still, last night had meant many things to Bridgette— and it wasn't all about the suave locum. Seeing her old colleagues, hearing about the midwifery unit, she'd realised just how much she was missing her old life. She knew somehow she had to get it back.

It was a curious thing that helped.

When Harry woke up at eleven and refused to go back to sleep, she held him as she checked her work sheet for the week. She was hoping that Courtney would be back tomorrow in time for her to get to her late shift when an e-mail pinged into her inbox.

No subject. No message. Just an attachment.

She had no idea how Dominic had got her e-mail

address, no idea at all, but she didn't dwell on it, just opened the attachment.

It didn't upset her to see it. In fact, it made her smile. She had no regrets for that night and the photo of them together proved it. The photo, not just of him but of herself smiling and happy, did more than sustain her—it inspired her.

'Harry Joyce,' she said to the serious face of her nephew. 'Your aunty Bridgette needs to get a life.'

And she *would* get one, Bridgette decided, carefully deleting Dominic's e-mail address so she didn't succumb, like Arabella, in the middle of the night. The photo, though, became her new screensaver.

CHAPTER FOUR

'HE'LL be fine.'

It was six-thirty a.m. on Monday morning and Bridgette's guilt didn't lift as she handed a very sleepy Harry over to Mary, whom she had been introduced to last week. 'It seems mean, waking him so early,' Bridgette said.

'Well, you start work early.' Mary had the same lovely Irish brogue as Bridgette's granny had had and was very motherly and practical. 'Is his mum picking him up?'

'No, it's just me for the next few days,' Bridgette explained. 'She's got laryngitis, so I'm looking after Harry for a while.'

'Now, I know you'll want to see him during your breaks and things, but I really would suggest that for the first week or two, you don't pop down. He will think you're there to take him home and will just get upset.' She gave Bridgette a nice smile. 'Which will upset you and you'll not get your work done for worrying. Maybe ring down if you want to know how he is, and of course if there are any problems and we need you, I'll be the first to let you know.' Holding Harry, Mary walked Bridgette to the door and gave her a little squeeze on the shoulder. 'You're doing grand.'

Oh, she wanted Mary to take her back to some mystical kitchen to sit at the table and drink tea for hours, for Mary to feed her advice about toddlers and tell her that everything was okay, was going to be okay, that Harry was fine.

Would be fine.

It felt strange to be back in her regular uniform, walking towards Maternity. Strange, but nice. It had been a busy month. She was so glad for that photo—their one night together had caused something of an awakening for Bridgette, had shown her just how much she was missing and had been the motivation to really sort her life out as best she could. She had been to the social-work department at the hospital she had once worked in and taken some much-needed advice. They suggested daycare and allocated Harry a place. At first Courtney had resisted. After all, she had said, she didn't work, but Bridgette stood firm—relieved that there would be more people looking out for Harry. She was especially glad that she had held her ground when the day before she started her new job, Courtney had come down with a severe throat infection and asked if Bridgette could step in for a few days.

Bridgette's interview with Rita had been long and rather difficult. Rita wasn't at all keen to make exceptions. She would do her best to give Bridgette early shifts but, no, she couldn't guarantee that was all she would get, and certainly, Rita said, she wanted all her staff to do regular stints on nights.

It all seemed a little impossible, but somehow Bridgette knew she had to make it work and get through things one day at a time—and today would be a good day, Bridgette decided as she entered the familiar unit, the smell and sound of babies in the air. This was where she belonged. She made herself a coffee to take into the long handover. Bridgette was hoping to be put into Labour and Delivery—she really wanted to immerse herself in a birth on her first day back.

'You're nice and early.' Rita was sitting at the computer, all busy and efficient and preparing for the day. 'Actually, that helps. It's been a very busy night, a busy weekend apparently. I've got a nurse who has to leave at seven. She's looking after a rather difficult case— would you mind taking handover from her and getting started?'

'Of course.' Bridgette was delighted. It often happened this way, and it would be lovely to get stuck into a labour on her first day back. She took a gulp of her coffee and tipped the rest down the sink, rinsed her cup and then headed off towards Labour and Delivery.

'No, it's room three where I want you to take over— twenty-four weeks with pre-eclampsia. They're having trouble getting her blood pressure back down.'

Okay, so she wasn't going to witness a birth this morning, but still, it was nice to be back using her midwifery brain. 'Hi, there, Heather.' She smiled at the familiar face. The room was quite crowded. Dr Hudson, the obstetrician, was there with the anaesthetist, and the anxious father was holding his wife's hand. The woman's face was flushed and she looked very drowsy. Thankfully, she was probably oblivious to all the activity going on.

'It's so good to see you.' Heather motioned to head to the door and they stepped just a little outside. 'I've got to get away at seven.'

'Is that why it's good to see me?' Bridgette smiled.

'No, it's just good to see you back, good to have someone on the ball taking over as well. I'm worried about this one. Her name is Carla. She came up from Emergency yesterday evening.' Heather gave Bridgette a detailed rundown, showing her all the drugs that had been used overnight in an attempt to bring Carla's blood pressure down. 'We thought we had it under control at four a.m., but at six it spiked again.' Bridgette grimaced when she saw the figures. 'Obviously, they were hoping for a few more days at the very least. She's supposed to be having a more detailed scan this morning. They were estimating twenty-four weeks and three days.' That was very early. Every day spent in the womb at this stage was precious and vital and would increase the baby's chance of survival.

The parents wanted active treatment and the mother had been given steroids yesterday to mature the baby's lungs in case of premature delivery, but even so, to deliver at this stage would be dire indeed. 'She's just been given an epidural,' Heather explained, 'and they're fiddling with her medications through that as well. They're doing everything they can to get her blood pressure down.' It just didn't seem to be working, though. The only true cure for pre-eclampsia was delivery. Carla's vital signs meant that her life was in danger. She was at risk of a stroke or seizures and a whole host of complications if she didn't stabilise soon—even death. 'They were just talking about transferring her over to Intensive Care, but I think Dr Hudson now wants to go ahead and deliver. The paediatrician was just in…he's warned them what to expect, but at that stage we were still hoping for a couple more days, even to get her to twenty-five weeks.'

It wasn't going to happen.

'I hate leaving her…'

'I know,' Bridgette said.

'Dillan starts at a new school today.' Bridgette knew Heather's son had had trouble with bullying and it sounded as if today was a whole new start for him too. 'Or I wouldn't dash off.'

'You need to get home.'

The monitors were beeping and Heather and Bridgette walked back in.

'Carla…' Heather roused the dozing woman. 'This is Bridgette. She's going to be taking care of you today, and I'll be back to take care of you tonight.'

The alarms were really going off now. The appalling numbers that the monitors were showing meant the difficult decision would have to be made. Bridgette knew that Heather was torn. She'd been with Carla all night and at any moment now Carla was going to be rushed over to Theatre for an emergency Caesarean. 'Go,' Bridgette mouthed, because if Heather didn't leave soon, she would surely end up staying, and Dillan needed his mum today.

'Let Theatre know we're coming over,' Dr Hudson said to Bridgette, 'and we need the crash team from NICU. I'll tell the parents.'

Bridgette dashed out and informed Rita, the smooth wheels of the emergency routine snapping into place. Five minutes to seven on a Monday was not the best time. Staff were leaving, staff were starting, the weekend team was exhausted, the corridors busy as they moved the bed over to the maternity theatres.

'Okay.' Bridgette smiled at the terrified father, whom Dr Hudson had agreed could be present for the birth. 'Here's where you get changed.' She gave him some scrubs, a hat and some covers for his shoes. 'I'm going to go and get changed too and then I'll come back for you and take you in.'

Really, her presence at this birth was somewhat supernumerary. For a normal Caesarean section she would be receiving the baby; however, the NICU team was arriving and setting up, preparing their equipment for this very tiny baby, so Bridgette concentrated on the parents. Frank, the husband, wanted to film the birth, and Bridgette helped him to work out where to stand so that he wouldn't get in the way. She understood his need to document every minute of this little baby's life.

'It's all happening so fast...' Carla, though groggy,

was clearly terrified, because now that the decision had been made, things were moving along with haste.

'We're just making sure we've got everything ready for your baby,' Bridgette explained as Dr Hudson came in. The anaesthetist had topped up the epidural and the operation would soon be starting.

'We're just waiting on...' Kelly, one of NICU team called out, when asked if they were ready, and then her voice trailed off. 'No problem. Dr Mansfield is here.'

Bridgette looked up and straight into those familiar black eyes, eyes that she stared at each day on her computer, except they didn't smile back at her now. She tore her gaze away from him and back to her patient. She completely halted her thoughts, gave all her attention to her patient, because the operation had started, the incision made at seven-eighteen, and just a few moments later a tiny baby was delivered.

'She's beautiful,' Bridgette told Carla. 'She's moving.' She was, her red, spindly limbs flailing with indignation at her premature entry to the world.

'She's not crying,' Jenny said.

'She is.' There was a very feeble cry and her face was grimacing. Frank was standing back, filming their tiny daughter. Bridgette watched the activity and for the first time she took a proper look at Dominic.

He needed to shave, his face was grim with concentration and he looked exhausted. Bridgette remembered Rita saying that it had been a very busy weekend, and this emergency had come right at the tail end of his on-call shift.

'Can I see her?' Carla asked, but already the team was moving the baby and she was whisked past. Carla got only a very brief glimpse.

'They're taking her into another area,' Bridgette explained, as the team moved away, 'and then she'll be taken up to the NICU.'

'Can I go with her?' Frank asked. 'Can I watch? I won't get in the way. I just want to see what they're doing.'

'I'll go and find out.'

Bridgette walked into the resuscitation area, where the baby would be stabilised as much as possible before being moved to NICU. Even though she had seen premature babies, now and for evermore the sight of something so small and so fragile and so completely tiny took her breath away. Bridgette loved big, fat babies, little scrawny ones too, but a scrap like this made her heart flutter in silent panic.

'She's a little fighter.' Kelly came over. 'We're going to move her up in a couple of minutes.'

'Dad wants to know if he can come and watch. He's promised not to get in the way. He just wants to see what's happening.'

'Not yet,' Dominic called over. 'I'll talk to him as soon as I can.'

'Tell him to stay with his wife for now,' Kelly suggested. 'I'll come and fetch him when Dominic is ready to talk to him.'

Kelly was as good as her word, and by the time Carla had been moved to Recovery, Kelly appeared, holding some new photos of their tiny daughter, which she handed to Mum and explained a little of what was going on. 'The doctors are still with her, but Dominic said if I bring Frank up he'll try to come out to speak with him. He'll come down and talk to you a bit later.'

It was a busy morning. Carla spent a long time in Recovery before being transferred back to the maternity unit, but even there she still required very close observation as her vital signs would take a while to stabilise after the birth. Carla was still very sick and of course wanted more information about her baby, whom they'd named Francesca. Frank had seen her very briefly and was now back with his wife and clearly a little impatient about the lack of news.

'Mary from daycare is on the phone for you.' Nandita, the ward clerk, popped a head around the door and handed Bridgette the phone.

'Nothing to worry about at all' came Mary's reassuring voice as Bridgette stepped out into the corridor. 'I'm just about to head off for lunch and I thought I'd let you know how well he's gone today. He's found a stack of bricks, which amused him for most of the morning.'

'Thanks so much for letting me know.'

'He's heading for an afternoon nap now. Anyway, you can get on with your day without fretting about him.' Bridgette felt a wave of guilt when she realised she hadn't even had time to worry about Harry and how he was doing on his first day at crèche and a wave of sadness too when she found out that, no, neither had Courtney rung to find out.

'Hi, Carla.' She gave the phone to Nandita, and as she walked back into her patient's room she heard Dominic's voice. If he had looked tired that morning then he looked exhausted now. 'Hi, Frank.' He shook the other man's hand. 'Sorry that it's taken so long to come and speak with you. I've been very busy with your daughter and another child who was delivered yesterday. I wanted to take the time to have a proper talk with you both.' He sat down next to the bed. 'Carla, you'll remember I spoke with you yesterday.' He didn't bog them down with too much detail. Apparently yesterday he had explained the risks of such a premature delivery and he didn't terrify them all over again. He told them their daughter's condition was extremely serious, but there was some good news. 'She seems a little further on than first estimated. I'd put her well into twenty-five weeks, which, though it's just a few days' difference, actually increases the survival rates quite dramatically. She's got size on her side too,' Dominic explained. 'Even though she's tiny, she is a little bit bigger than we would expect at twenty-five weeks, and she's had the benefit of the steroids we gave yesterday. She's a vigorous little thing, and she's doing absolutely as well as can be expected.'

'When can I see her?' Carla asked.

'I spoke to Dr Hudson before I came down, and as much as we know you want to see your daughter, you're not well enough at the moment.'

'What if…?' Poor Carla didn't even want to voice it, so Dominic did.

'If her condition deteriorates, we'll sort something out and do our best to get you up there.' He glanced over at Bridgette and so too did Carla.

'Of course we will,' she said.

'But right now the best you can do for your baby is to rest and get well yourself.' He answered a few more questions and then turned to Frank. 'You should be able to see her for a little while now. I've told them to expect you.'

'I'll get Nandita to walk you up,' Bridgette offered.

'Lunch?' Rita suggested as Bridgette walked over to speak with Nandita. 'Emma will take over from you.'

It was a late lunch, and as Bridgette hadn't had a coffee break, it was a sheer relief to slip off her shoes and just relax for a few moments. Well, at least it was until Dominic came in and sat on the couch opposite and unwrapped a roll. He gave her a brief nod but did not make any attempt at conversation, instead choosing to read a newspaper. It was Bridgette who tried to tackle the uncomfortable silence.

'I thought you were in Sydney.'

'It didn't work out.' He carried on reading the paper for a moment and then finally elaborated a touch. 'The professor I would be working under was taken ill and has gone on long-term sick leave—I didn't really care for his replacement, so I'm just waiting till something I want comes up, or the professor returns. I'm here for a few more weeks.'

He sounded very austere, such a contrast to the easy conversations they had once shared. He didn't say anything else, didn't even read his paper, just sat and ate his roll.

Couldn't he have done that on NICU or on the paed ward? Bridgette thought, stirring her yoghurt. If he was going to sit there all silent and brooding, couldn't he do it somewhere else? Surely it was already awkward enough?

For Dominic, in that moment, it wasn't awkward, not in the least. He was too busy concentrating on not closing his eyes. Fatigue seeped through him. He'd had maybe six hours' sleep the entire weekend and he just wanted to go home and crash. Thank goodness for Rita, who had noticed his pallor and given him a spare cold patient lunch and suggested that he take five minutes before he saw the baby he had come down to examine, as well as speaking with Frank and Carla. Rebecca, his intern, came in. Bridgette recognised her from that morning, and then a couple of other colleagues too, which should have broken the tension, but instead Dominic ignored everyone and made no attempt to join in with the chitchat.

And later, he didn't look up when she had no choice but to sit and join him at the nurses' station to write up her notes before going home.

He told, rather than asked, Rebecca to take some further bloods on a baby born over the weekend, and then when one of the midwives asked if he'd mind taking a look at some drug orders, holding out the prescription chart to him, he didn't take it. Rather rudely, Bridgette thought, he didn't even look up.

'Is it a patient of mine?'

'No, it's a new delivery.'

He just carried on writing his own notes. 'Then you need to ring the doctor on call.'

The midwife rolled her eyes and left them to it, and the silence simmered uncomfortably between them, or at least it was uncomfortable for Bridgette.

'I'm sorry this is awkward.' She tried to broach it, to go ahead and say what was surely on both their minds, to somehow ease the tension, because the Dominic she had seen today was nothing like the man she had met, and she certainly didn't want to cause any problems at work. 'Had I known you were still working here, I wouldn't have…' Her voice trailed off—it seemed rather stupid to say that she'd never have taken the job, that she wouldn't have come back to the unit she loved. But had she known he would be here for a little while more, there might have been a delay in her return—with Jasmine being away she was completely out of the loop as to what was going on at work.

'Awkward?' Dominic frowned as he carried on writing. 'Why would it be awkward?' And then he shook his head. 'Are you referring to…?' He looked over and waited till her skin was burning, till there was no question that, yes, she was referring to that night. 'Bridgette, it was months ago.' She swallowed, because it was actually just a few weeks; she'd counted them. 'We shared one night together.' How easily he dismissed it, relegated it, reduced it to a long-ago event that had meant nothing—something so trivial that it didn't even merit a moment's reflection. Except she was quite sure that wasn't true.

'Thanks for the e-mail,' she said, to prove it had been more than that, that he had come back to her door, had later that night sent her a photo, yet he frowned as if trying to place it and then he had the nerve to give a wry laugh.

'Oh, that!'

'You got my e-mail address?'

'On some stupid group one from Vince and...' He gave a shrug, clearly couldn't remember Jasmine's name. 'Just clearing out my inbox, Bridgette.' She felt like a stalker, some mad, obsessed woman, and he clearly must be thinking the same. 'It was one night— hardly something to base your career path on. Don't give it another thought. There really is no problem.'

'Good.'

'And as for awkward, it's not in the least. This is how I am at work.' And then he corrected himself. 'This is how I am—ask anyone.' He gave a very thin smile. 'I'm not exactly known for small talk. It has nothing to do with what took place. It really is forgotten.'

And over the next few days he proved his point. She saw that Dr Dominic Mansfield *was* cool and dis-tant with everyone. He was mainly polite, sometimes dismissive, and just never particularly friendly. There was an autonomous air to him that wasn't, Bridgette realised, solely reserved for her. Not that she should mind—nothing had shifted her heart. She was still way too raw to contemplate a relationship. And the patients, or rather their parents, didn't seem to mind the directness of his words in the least. In fact, as Bridgette wheeled Carla up later in the week for a visit with her newborn, Carla admitted it was Dr Mansfield's opinion she sought the most about her daughter.

'I don't want a doctor who tries to spare my feelings,' Carla said as they waited for the lift. 'He tells it like it is, which Frank and I appreciate.

'Mind you...' she smiled as Bridgette wheeled her in '...he's not exactly chatty. Gorgeous to look at he may be, but you wouldn't want to be stuck in a lift with him.' Whether she agreed or not, Bridgette smiled back, pleased to see her patient's humour returning, along with colour to her cheeks. It really had been a hellish ride for Carla. It had been four days until she had been well enough to see her baby, and there was still, for Francesca, a long road ahead.

'Carla.' Dominic gave a nod to the patient as Bridgette wheeled her over.

'Is everything okay?' Carla asked, anxious to see him standing by Francesca's incubator.

'She's had a good morning, by all reports,' Dominic said. 'I'm just checking in.'

He gave Bridgette the briefest nod of acknowledgement then moved on to the next incubator. He wasn't, she now realised, being rude or dismissive towards her. It was the way Dominic was to everyone.

It hurt more than she had time to allocate to it. Her days were so busy, and more and more Courtney was asking her to have Harry. It was hard trying to achieve some sort of routine and work full-time with a toddler—a toddler who worryingly didn't toddle very much, one who seemed far happier to sit with his building blocks, happier in his own world than hers. But sometimes at night, when all she should do was close her eyes and get some much-needed sleep, it was then that Bridgette's mind wandered. It was on those occasions that she realised not so much what she'd lost but more what she'd been privy to that night.

A side to Dominic that was rare indeed.

CHAPTER FIVE

'HARRY!' Bridgette gave him a wide smile but Harry didn't look up. He was engrossed with the pile of bricks in front of him. 'How has he been today?' Bridgette asked.

'Busy building!' Mary answered. 'He loves his bricks.'

Bridgette saw her own fingers clench around the pen as she signed Harry out for the day, saw the white of her knuckles as her brain tightened just a fraction, wondering if Mary's comment was friendly chatter or a more professional observation. She was being paranoid, Bridgette told herself, seeing problems where there were surely none, but as she picked up Harry she wished, and not for the first time, that Harry was just a little bit more pleased to see her, a little more receptive.

There couldn't be something wrong with him. It wasn't just for selfish reasons that she panicked at the thought—it was Courtney's reaction that troubled Bridgette, or rather Courtney's lack of reaction towards her son. Her sister wasn't exactly coping now, let alone if her son had special needs.

Special needs.

It was the first time that she had actually said it, even if only in her mind, and instantly she shoved it aside because there was just so much to deal with at the moment. She had so many things to contend with, without adding the unthinkable to the pile. But she had to approach it.

'How do you think he's doing?' she asked Mary.

'Grand.' She beamed. 'Mind, he does have a bit of a temper—' she tickled him under the chin '—if one of the other littlies knocks over his bricks.'

'What about his talking?' Bridgette looked at Mary, who just smiled at Harry.

'He's not much of a talker,' Mary said, 'but, then, he's just been here a couple of weeks and is still settling in so maybe he's a bit shy. If you're concerned, though…' Mary was lovely, but she told Bridgette what she already knew, that maybe his mum should take him to his GP if she was worried that he wasn't reaching his milestones.

'How is Mum?' Mary asked, because, despite Courtney collecting him a couple of times, it mainly fell to Bridgette.

'She's okay,' Bridgette answered. 'Though I'll be bringing Harry in for the next couple of days. She's got some job interviews lined up in Bendigo and is staying there with friends for a few nights.'

'Bendigo!' Mary's eyebrows rose. 'That's a good few hours away.'

'Well, it's early days,' Bridgette said, 'but it's good that she's looking for work.'

Bridgette had mixed feelings. Yes, she wanted her sister to get a job and to make a fresh start, but the thought of her, or rather Harry, so far away had Bridgette in a spin. She was doing her best not to dwell on it as she left the crèche.

'Excuse me!' She heard the irritation in the man's voice as she, a woman who wasn't looking where she was going, collided with him as she walked out of the daycare centre. And then Dominic looked down, saw who he was talking to, saw who she was holding, and she was quite sure that he frowned as he gazed into Harry's eyes. Eyes that were exactly the same sludgy grey as hers, and though he quickly moved his features to impassive and gave her a very brief nod, she could feel the tension. They walked down a long corridor, Bridgette several steps behind him. As he headed out through the ambulance bay and turned left, it was clear they were both heading for the car park.

She should have managed to avoid him, given that she now walked incredibly slowly, but one of the security guards halted him and they spoke for a moment. No matter how Bridgette dawdled, no matter how hard she tried not to catch up, the security guard gave him a cheery farewell at the very second Bridgette walked past and, like it or not, for a moment or two there was no choice but to fall in step alongside him.

'Is that why you had to dash off?'

It was the first time he acknowledged he even *recalled* the details of that night, that morning, the slice of time when things had felt more than right.

'I should have explained…' She really didn't know what to say, what could she say. 'I didn't know how…' She still didn't. Should she plead, 'I'm his aunt. He's not my responsibility'? Harry was, he was solid in her arms—and whether Harry understood her words or not, he certainly did not need to be present as she defended her reasons for not telling this man of his existence. Instead she walked to her car that, unlike his, which lit up like a Christmas tree the second he approached, needed keys. Bridgette had to scrabble in her bag for them, with Harry, who was becoming increasingly heavy, but she was too nervous to put him down in the middle of a car park. He was, she realised, just too precious to let go.

As Dominic's sleek silver car slid past her, she deliberately did not look up, did not want to remember the night he'd driven her to heaven then returned her home again.

She was very close to crying, and that Harry did not need, but finally she found her keys and unlocked the car, opening the windows to let it cool down before she put Harry in.

'Here we go.' The car still felt like a sauna but she strapped Harry in, climbed into the seat and looked in the rear-vision mirror at his wispy curls and serious grey eyes. She gave him a very nice smile. 'You're ruining my love life, Harry!'

CHAPTER SIX

'Wow!' Bridgette walked into the delivery room, where Maria was pacing. 'I turn my back for five minutes…' She smiled at Maria, who had progressed rapidly in the past half hour.

'I was worried you wouldn't make it back,' Maria said.

'I'm sorry I had to dash off.' Harry had been a touch grizzly this morning when she'd dropped him off and had, half an hour ago, thrown the most spectacular temper tantrum, bad enough for Mary to call her on the ward and for Bridgette to take an early coffee break.

'I know what it's like,' Maria said. 'I've got three of my own.'

'Four soon,' Bridgette said, and Maria smiled.

'I can't wait to meet her.'

'Neither can I,' Bridgette admitted. It was, so far, turning out to be a gorgeous labour—especially as it was one that could have been labelled 'difficult' because the testing and scans had revealed that Maria and Tony's baby had Trisomy 21. The diagnosis, Maria had told Bridgette, had caused intense upset between both families—Spanish passion combined with pointless accusations and blame had caused a lot of tension and heartache indeed. Maria and Tony, however, once they had got over the initial shock, had researched as much as they could, and had even met with a local support group who ran a regular playgroup.

'It took away a lot of the fear,' Maria had explained, when Bridgette admitted her. 'Seeing other Down's syndrome babies and toddlers and their parents coping so well. We're so looking forward to having our baby. I just wish our families would stop with the grief.'

So upset was Maria with the response of her family that she hadn't even wanted them to know that she had gone into labour, but with three other small children to care for she'd had no choice but to tell them. And now two anxious families were sitting in the maternity waiting room. Still, Maria was doing beautifully and was helped so much by her husband's unwavering support. He rubbed her back where she indicated, stopped talking when she simply raised a hand. They had their own private language and were working to deliver their daughter as a team.

'How are things?' Rita popped her head around the door. 'The family just asked for an update.'

'It's all going well,' Bridgette said.

'Tell them it will be born when it's good and ready,' Maria snapped, and then breathed through another contraction. She was suddenly savage. 'You'd think they were preparing for a funeral more than a birth!' She let out an expletive or three in Spanish and Tony grimaced, then she told him *exactly* what she thought of Abuela.

'Grandmother,' Tony translated with a smile when Bridgette winked at him. 'My mother.' He rolled his eyes. 'She does a lot for us, but she can be a bit too much at times, though she means well.' He rubbed his wife's back as Maria said a little more of what she thought about her mother-in-law. 'Maria always does this when…' And Bridgette smiled, knew as Tony did, what was coming. Maria leant against the bed, her face changing to a familiar grimace.

'I want to push.'

'That's good,' Bridgette cheered.

'Come on, Tony,' she said and they both helped Maria up onto the bed. 'I'm just going to let Dr Hudson know—'

'No need.' Dr Hudson came in.

'How's she doing?' Rita popped her head around the door again and Bridgette gritted her teeth, while trying not to let Maria see.

'Can we get the paediatrician down?' The obstetrician's tone was a little brusque and Bridgette saw the flare of panic in Maria's eyes.

'It's fine, Maria,' Bridgette reassured her as Rita went to make the call. 'The fact Dr Hudson wants the paediatrician to come down means that you're getting close now and it won't be long till your baby's born.'

'The paediatrician is on his way,' Rita called over the intercom. 'I'll come in and give you a hand in a moment.'

Bridgette watched as Maria's eyes closed; as she dipped into her own private world and just tried to block the gathering crowd out. She had wanted the birth to be as low-key and as relaxed as possible, and had three other births with which to compare, but because of the possible health complications, more staff would be present with this one. Though potentially necessary, it just compounded things for Maria.

'Have you got everything ready?' Rita bustled into the room. 'Dominic is just a couple of minutes away.'

Bridgette felt incredibly confident with Dominic. He was an amazing doctor and very astute. However, for Maria, perhaps it was not the best combination of staff. Dr Hudson believed in planning for every eventuality—*every* eventuality—and Rita was one of those high-energy people who somehow didn't soothe. Now Dominic, a rather aloof paediatrician, was being added to the mix, except… 'Dominic Mansfield?' Tony looked over at Bridgette. 'Is that the paediatrician who's coming?' When Bridgette nodded, Tony hugged his wife. 'That's good news, Maria.'

'Bridgette?' Rita was checking and double-checking everything Bridgette had already done. 'Have you got the—?'

'Shut up!' roared Maria, just as Dominic came into the room.

For once Bridgette was grateful for his silence. He gave Tony a nod as Maria quietly laboured. Dominic took off his jacket and headed to the sink to wash his hands and then tied on a plastic apron.

'Big breath, Maria,' Bridgette said gently. 'Come on, another one…' The birth was imminent. 'And then push until Dr Hudson tells you to stop.' Maria was very good at this. There was grim concentration on her face as she bore down and Bridgette held her leg, relaying Dr Hudson's gruff instructions but in more encouraging tones. 'Don't push now. Just breathe. The head's out.'

The baby didn't even require another push. She slithered out into Dr Hudson's hands, where Rita was waiting to cut the cord and whisk the baby off for examination.

'Up onto Mum's stomach,' Dominic said. 'Tony can cut the cord.' Bridgette silently cheered as his calm, authoritative voice slowed the haste.

'Do you want the baby moved over for examination?' Rita checked when, again, she didn't need to. It had been a very beautiful birth, and Bridgette was especially thrilled that Dominic seemed in no rush to whisk the baby off and examine her—instead, he just quietly observed.

The little girl was small and Bridgette placed a towel over her, rubbing her to stimulate her, but she felt very calm with Dominic's stoic presence so close.

As the baby took her first breaths, Dominic called Tony over and the cord was cut—and Bridgette felt a blink of tears because the birth Maria had wanted so badly for her baby was happening.

'I can examine her here,' Dominic said, when Rita checked again if he wanted the baby moved over. And he did. He checked the little baby's muscle tone and her palate and listened to her heart for a long time. He told Maria he would perform a more comprehensive examination in a little while. 'But for now I'll let you enjoy her.'

There really was a lot to enjoy. She peered up at her mum, her almond-shaped eyes huge and gorgeous; she was very alert, and even though she let out a few little cries, she was easily comforted by Maria.

'Do you want me to let your family know?' Rita asked, and Bridgette's jaw tightened. She could understand the conversation that had been held at Jasmine's leaving do now. Rita really did try and take over.

'They'll want to come in,' Maria said. 'I just don't want...' She held her baby closely. 'I want it to be a celebration, the same as it was with my others.'

'It will be,' Dominic said. 'They just haven't met her yet.'

'She wants to feed,' Maria said, as her daughter frantically searched for her breast.

'Let her.'

'You said they'd scan her first,' Maria said, because, though detailed prenatal scans had not shown anything, the nature of the syndrome meant the little girl was at risk of a heart defect and would need to be checked by a paediatric cardiologist soon after birth, but Dominic was clearly happy with his findings.

'She's looking great,' he said, quietly observing, and the baby did latch on, but Bridgette helped with the positioning.

It was one of those births that confirmed her vocation—there was no greater gift than watching a new life come into the world, and today's so-called difficult birth had been made especially wonderful by the calm presence of Dominic. Again he had surprised her. He wasn't particularly effusive or gushing, he was so much *more* than that, and he was everything this little family needed today.

Dominic stayed and wrote up his notes while the little girl fed and Bridgette watched for any signs that the baby was having trouble sucking and swallowing but she was doing very well. 'Dominic said that breast feeding might be more difficult than with the others…' Maria looked down at her daughter, who was tiring, so Bridgette suggested she take her off now.

'She's doing an awful lot right,' Bridgette said, checking the babe and then filling in her own notes. 'She's cried, pooed, wee'd and fed.'

Dominic came over. 'You remember I said that I'd take her up to NICU for a little while after she was born,' he said. 'I want that scan done. Everything looks good,' he reassured the parents, 'but I just want her thoroughly checked. Hopefully she'll be back down with you soon.'

Maria nodded and then took a deep breath. 'Can you bring in my family first?' Her eyes went to her husband's. 'If they start, I want you to…'

'We'll be here,' Bridgette said. 'You won't have to say a thing. I'm very good at bringing up excuses as to why people have to leave. If you start getting upset, or you've just had enough, you just have to let me know.'

They worked out a little code, and she gave Tony a smile as he walked out. Dominic, she noted, instead of heading out to the desk, was sitting on a couch in the corner of the room, finishing his notes—a quiet, unobtrusive presence that was welcome.

Maria and Tony set the tone, but Bridgette's heart did go out to the family. They were trying to be brave, to not be upset, but there was so much tension, so many questions as they all peered at the newest member of the clan. Then Maria's three-year-old, Roman, climbed up on the bed and gazed at his sister, kissing her on the forehead, and the old *abuela* laughed.

Dominic came over and checked the baby briefly again, more for the family's benefit, or rather Maria's, Bridgette rightly guessed, because the questions they had been asking Maria were aimed at him now.

'She's doing very, very well,' he said, and answered more of their questions and told them that, yes, the prenatal diagnosis was correct. Yes, shortly there would be further testing, but for now she was doing perfectly. And then Bridgette blinked as he chatted with the *abuela* in what appeared to be fluid Spanish for a moment. *'Sí, ella es perfecta...'*

'We're going to move her up now.' Kelly from NICU had come down just as all the cameras came out.

'Photo with *el medico*,' the *abuela* said.

'We really ought to get moving.' Dominic was reluctant, but then obliged, and it struck Bridgette that though of course he held babies in the course of examining them, he wasn't the type to steal a cuddle.

He held the new infant and gave a smile for the camera and then he looked down at her.

'She's gorgeous, isn't she?' Maria said.

'Oh, I don't do the cute-baby thing,' Dominic answered, 'but, yes, I think I have to agree in this case. You have a very cute baby. Has she got a name?'

'Esperanza,' Maria said.

'Hope!' Dominic smiled.

He popped her back in her cot and at the last minute Tony asked if he might be able to stay with the baby during her tests. When Dominic agreed, the family all followed Dominic, Kelly and the porters in a little procession down the hall.

'He's lovely, isn't he?' Maria said. 'Dominic, I mean. He sort of tells you like it is.'

'He's very good,' Bridgette said, and gave Maria a wink. 'Speaks Spanish too.'

'Abuela was very impressed.' Maria grinned. 'Dominic's mother is Spanish apparently.' She had to find out about him from a patient! 'He's been great. We went to him when we got the amnio back and he told us what to expect. Well, I guess he'd know as his brother has Down's.' She must have seen Bridgette's eyes widen. 'Sorry, maybe I shouldn't have said—it was just that Tony was crying and so was I and it seemed like a disaster when we first found out, but Dominic was terribly patient. He told us what we were feeling was completely normal. We saw him again a couple of weeks ago and we were embarrassed about the scene we'd made, but he said not to give it another thought. It was all very normal, that his mother had been the same.'

They knew nothing about each other, Bridgette realised.

Which had been the point, she remembered.

She really was lousy at one-night stands.

Still, she didn't have time to dwell on it. L and D was busy and she was soon looking after another birth, a first-time mum called Jessica, who was very nervous, as well as keeping an eye on Maria.

Esperanza was gone for about an hour, and her heart test was clear, which was brilliant news, and by the time she was back, Bridgette had just transferred Maria to the ward. Having checked on her next patient, Bridgette was more than ready for lunch.

'What's all this?' Bridgette tried not to care that Dominic was sitting in the staffroom. After all, if he didn't care, why should she? Anyway, Rita was there too and there were other distractions this lunchtime. Instead of plain biscuits the table was heaving with fruit platters, small filled rolls and a spread of cheese.

'Leftovers from the obstetricians' meeting.' Rita gave a wry smile. 'I rescued some for the workers. Enjoy.'

Bridgette selected a roll and a few slivers of fruit. She glanced at the cheese—even though that would usually be her first option, even if it seemed stupid, with Dominic there she chose to give it a miss.

'How's Harry?' Rita asked.

'Better,' Bridgette answered. 'He was just having a

bit of a tantrum. He's not in the best of moods today.
I'm sorry I had to dash off.'

As annoying and inflexible as she could be, Rita
could, Bridgette conceded, also be very nice. 'No problem. It's to be expected in the first weeks at daycare.
He'll soon get used to it. The real question is, how is
his aunt doing?'

'Trying to get used to it too,' Bridgette admitted.
'But we're getting there.'

Unfortunately Rita's break was soon over and word
couldn't yet have got around about the spread on in
the staffroom because only Dominic and Bridgette remained. Well, she wasn't going to give up a single minute of the precious break by going back early. Her feet
were killing her and she was hungry too, and Jessica,
her new patient, was progressing steadily. If Dominic
wasn't feeling awkward then why on earth should she
be? And if she wanted cheese, why not?

Bridgette stood and refilled her plate with some
Cheddar and Brie and a few crackers and went to sit
back down, selecting a magazine to read as she did so.

'I thought you liked blue cheese.'

'Maybe.' Bridgette refused to look up, just carried
on reading the magazine. She was not going to jump to
make conversation just because he suddenly deigned to
do so.

'How's Maria?'

'Marvellous.' She refused to be chatty, just because
he suddenly was.

'The baby I saw you with yesterday...' Still she did

not fill in the spaces. 'He's your nephew?' When still
he was met with silence, Dominic pushed a little further. 'Why didn't you just say so?'

'I don't really see that it's relevant,' Bridgette answered, still reading her magazine. 'Had our one-night
stand been two years ago and you'd seen me walking out
of daycare carrying a mini-Dominic, then, yes, perhaps
I'd have had some explaining to do. But I don't.' She
smirked with mild pleasure at her choice of words and
looked up. She was rather surprised to see that he was
smiling—not the Dr Mansfield smile that she had seen
occasionally since her return to work but the Dominic
smile she had once been privy to.

'I'm sorry about yesterday. I just jumped to conclu-
sions. I saw you with—' he paused for a brief second
'—Harry, and I thought that was the reason...' He really felt awkward, Bridgette realised. Despite insisting
how easy this was, Dominic seemed to be struggling.

'The reason?' She frowned, because he'd done this
to her too, made her blush as she'd revealed that she
thought about that night—but Dominic didn't blush in
the same way Bridgette had.

'The reason that you went home that morning.'

'Oh, I needed a reason, did I?' She went back to her
magazine.

What was it with this woman? She had made it very
clear that morning that she didn't want more than their
one night. Normally it would have come as a relief to
Dominic, an unusual relief because he was not the one
working out how to end things.

'Excuse me.' Her phone buzzed in her pocket and Bridgette pulled it out, taking a deep breath before answering.

'Hi, Mum.'

Why did he have to be here when she took this call? Hopefully he'd choose now to leave, but instead he just sat there.

'I might need a hand a little bit later,' she said to her mother. She'd left a message for her parents earlier in the day, when she'd realised that Harry might not last out the day in crèche and also she wanted to stay longer for Jessica. 'There's a chance that I won't be able to get away for work on time and it would really help if you could pick up Harry at four for me.' She closed her eyes as her mother gave the inevitable reply. 'Yes, I know the crèche doesn't close till six, but he's a bit grizzly today and I don't want to push things—it's been a long day for him.'

Bridgette looked down and realised she was clicking her pen on and off as her mother reeled out her excuses. She could hear the irritation creeping into her own voice as she responded. 'I know Dad's got the dentist but can't he go on his own?' She listened to the train of excuses, to how they would love to help, but how nervous Dad got at the dentist, and if he did need anything done when they got there… 'You mean he's just having a check-up?' Now Bridgette couldn't keep the exasperation from her voice. She really wanted to be there for Jessica and didn't want to be nervously keeping one eye on the clock in case the crèche rang.

With a pang that she didn't want to examine, her heart ached for the long day Harry was having. She wanted some back-up, and despite her parents' constant reassurances that they would help, she never seemed to ask at the right time.

'Don't worry about it' Bridgette settled for, and managed a goodbye and then clicked off the phone. Then she couldn't help it—she shot out a little of the frustration that her parents so easily provoked. 'Why can't he go to the dentist by himself?' Bridgette asked as Dominic simply grinned at her exasperation. 'They go shopping together, they do the housework together… I mean, are they joined at the hip? Honestly, they don't do anything by themselves.'

'Breathe.' Dominic grinned and she did as the doctor recommended, but it didn't help and she stamped her feet for a moment and let out a brief 'Aagggh!'

'Better?' Dominic asked.

'A bit.'

Actually, she did feel a bit better. It was nice to have a little moan, to complain, to let some of her exasperation out. Her parents had always been the same—everything revolved around dinner, everything in the house was geared towards six p.m. They were so inflexible, right down to the brand of toothpaste they used, and that was fine, that was how it was, that was how they were, but right now Bridgette needed more hands and their four seemed to make a poor two.

'Have you got no one else who can help?' Dominic asked.

'I miss Jasmine for things like this,' Bridgette admitted. It was nice that they were finally talking but of course now that they were, Rita buzzed and told her Jessica was in transition and it was time for her to go back.

'You might be out by four,' he said, and she shook her head, because Jessica was a first-time mum.

'I doubt it.'

Dominic's phone was ringing as she left, and when he saw that it was his father, he chose not to answer it. Stupid, really, because his father would just ring again in an hour, Dominic thought, and every hour after that, till he could tick it off his to-do list.

He finally took the call at three.

'Hi.'

Dominic rolled his eyes as his father wished him a happy birthday. 'Thanks.' Dominic was being honest when he said that he couldn't talk for long, because he was summoned urgently and headed down to Theatre when paged for a child who was having an allergic reaction in Recovery. There was that theatre nurse, her blue eyes waiting, when he and the anaesthetist had finished discussing the child's care.

'Long shift?' Dominic asked when she yawned, because on certain occasions he did make conversation.

And today was a certain occasion.

It was, after all, his birthday.

'It's been busy.' She nodded.

'Back again in the morning?'

'Yes...though I shouldn't moan. My husband's away so I can just go home and sleep.'

He was always away, Dominic thought.

'What does he do?' He broke one of their rules and he watched her cheeks go pink. There were colleagues around, and they were seemingly just chatting, so of course she had to answer.

'He drives a coach,' Blue Eyes said. 'Overnight, Melbourne to Sydney.'

He gave a nod and walked off, felt a bit sick in the guts really, which wasn't like him, but he thought of the poor bloke driving up and down the freeway as Dominic bonked his wife. No questions asked, no real conversation.

Maybe he was growing up, Dominic thought. He hadn't been with anyone in weeks, not since Bridgette, in fact, though he rapidly shoved that thought out of his mind.

Well, why wouldn't he be growing up? It was his birthday, after all.

And birthdays were supposed to be enjoyed.

Never doubt the power of a woman in labour—Bridgette should really have known better. Jessica was amazing, focused and gritty, and the birth was wonderful, so wonderful that she was still high on adrenaline as she sped down the corridor to daycare.

'Bridgette.' He was walking towards her and this time he nodded *and* said her name—progress indeed!

'Dominic.' She grinned and nodded back at him,

ready to keep walking, except he stopped in front of her.

'I was wondering,' Dominic said. 'Would you like to come out tonight? You're right, this is awkward, and I'd really like to clear the air.'

This she hadn't been expecting. 'The air is already clear, Dominic.' Except it wasn't, so Bridgette was a little more honest. 'You were right. Harry is the reason that I didn't want you to come in that first night. My computer didn't have a virus.' She gave a guilty grin. 'Well, it wasn't Harry exactly, more the cot and the stroller and the rather blatant clues that were littered around my flat at the time.' And with Bridgette, he did ask questions, and got some answers. 'I look after my nephew a lot. My sister's really young.' He didn't look away, his eyes never left her face, and she rather wished that they would. 'So!' She gave him a smile as his pager went off and Dominic glanced down at it and then switched it off. 'That's a little bit what my life is like when Harry's with my sister—I'm permanently on call.' Yes, the air had been cleared, and now they could both move on; she truly wasn't expecting what came next.

'Bridgette, would you like to come out tonight?'

She turned around slowly and he looked the same as he had before—completely unreadable. She didn't want a charity dinner, didn't want him taking her out because he'd already asked her. To make things easier for them both she gave him a small smile, shook her head and politely declined. 'That's really nice of you, thanks, but I have to say no—it's hard to get a baby-sitter.' There, she'd given him the out. It was over and done with, and she awaited his polite smile back—it didn't come. Instead he looked at his watch.

'How long does a dental check-up take?' He even smiled. 'Can you try?' He pulled out a card and wrote his mobile-phone number on it and handed it to her. Maybe he read her too well because instead of saying that he would wait to hear if she could make arrangements, he lobbed the ball firmly back into her court. 'I'll pick you up at seven, unless I hear otherwise. Ring me if you can't get a babysitter.'

It was utterly and completely unexpected. She had thought he would run a mile—she'd given him an out, after all.

She wanted him to take it.

Bridgette really did. She just wasn't ready to get back out there and certainly not with Dominic. Still, maybe tonight he would just tell her how impossible it all was; maybe she would receive a long lecture on how they found each other attractive and all that, but how unsuitable they were—yet, remembering just how good they had been, it was very hard to say no.

'Hi, Mum.' It was the second time that day she'd asked her mum for help. 'Is there any chance you and Dad could babysit tonight?'

'You mean have our grandson over?' Betty laughed. 'We'd love to.' As Bridgette blinked in surprise, as she paused just a fraction, her mother filled the gap. 'Though we do have a couple of friends coming over tonight. Old friends of your dad's—remember Eric and Lorna?' Bridgette felt her jaw tense. Her parents insisted they were accommodating, but it was always on their terms—when it suited them. 'Could we maybe do it tomorrow?'

'I've got an invitation to go out tonight, Mum. I'd really like to go.'

'But we've got people over tonight. Tomorrow we can come over to you and stay. It might be easier on Harry.' Yes, it might be easier on Harry, but it certainly wouldn't be easier on her—or Dominic. He was already taking a leap of faith in asking her out. Though he wasn't asking her out, she reminded herself—he simply wanted to clear the air. Still, no doubt he was used to having the door opened by a groomed, glossy beauty who invited him in for a drink as she applied a final layer of lip gloss—somehow she couldn't imagine inflicting her mother and father and Harry on the guy.

'Mum, I haven't had a night out in weeks.' She hadn't, not since that night with Dominic. 'I'm sorry for the short notice. If you can have Harry, that would be great. If not…' If not, then it simply wasn't meant to be, Bridgette decided. If she couldn't get away for one single night without planning it days in advance, she might just as well text Dominic now with the whole truth.

It would be quite a relief to, actually, but after a moment's silence came her mother's rather martyred response. 'Well, make sure you bring a decent change of clothes for him. I want Harry looking smart. I've got

Eric and Lorna coming over,' she repeated. 'Have you had his hair cut yet?' Bridgette looked at the mop of blond curls that danced in the afternoon sun as Harry built his bricks and wondered why her mother assumed that Harry's hair was Bridgette's responsibility. His mop of unruly hair was a slight bone of contention between them—Courtney would never think to get a haircut for her son and though at first it had irritated Bridgette, more and more his wild curls suited him. Bridgette was now reluctant to get them cut—she certainly wasn't going to rush out and get a haircut just to appease her parents' guests and, anyway, there wasn't time. 'No, Courtney hasn't had his hair cut, but he's looking beautiful and I've got a gorgeous outfit for him.'

And with Harry dropped off and the quickest bath in history taken, the flat had to be hastily tidied, not that she had any intention of Dominic coming in. She'd be ready and dressed at the door, Bridgette decided, so she had about sixteen minutes to work out a not-so-gorgeous outfit for herself.

There was a grey shift dress at the back of her wardrobe and she had to find her ballet pumps but first she had a quick whiz with hair tongs and her magical blusher.

'Please be late,' she begged as she remembered her screensaver was of them. Her computer was in the spare bedroom, but in case of earthquake and it was the room they ended up in, she had to change it.

'Please be late,' she said again as she stashed dishes

in the cupboard beneath the sink and shovelled piles of building bricks into the corner.

'Please be late,' she said as she opened her bedroom door to get her pumps and was distracted by the shelves she'd been meaning to build and the million-thread-count sheets she'd bought in a sale and had been saving for when the room was painted.

But the bedroom was too untidy to even contemplate bringing him in and, no, her prayers weren't answered.

Bang on seven, she heard the doorbell.

CHAPTER SEVEN

'READY!' Bridgette beamed as she opened the front door and stepped out, because there was no way he was coming in.

'Shoes?' Dominic helpfully suggested just after she closed the door.

'Oh. Yes.' Which meant she had to rummage in her bag for her keys as he stood there. 'They must be in here.'

'Can't the babysitter let you in?'

'He's at my parents',' she said as she rummaged.

'Have you locked yourself out?'

'No, no,' Bridgette said cheerfully. 'I do this all the time—here they are.' She produced them with a 'ta ra!' and she let herself in, which of course meant that she had to let him in too—well, she couldn't really leave him on the doorstep.

'Go through,' she said, because she didn't even want him to get a glimpse of the chaos in the bedroom. 'I'll just be a moment.' Except he didn't go through. He stood in the hallway as she slipped through the smallest crack in the door and then scrambled to find her shoes. She must get more organised. Bridgette knew that, dreamt of the day when she finally had some sort of routine. She'd had a loose one once, before Harry was born, but now the whole flat seemed to have gone to pot.

There they were, under the bed. She grabbed her pumps and sort of limbo-danced around the door so that he wouldn't see inside. 'Sorry about that,' she said. 'Just been a bit of a mad rush.'

'Look, if you're too tired to go out for dinner…'

She gave him a strange look. 'I'm starving,' Bridgette said. 'How could anyone be too tired to eat dinner?'

'I meant…'

'So we're not going out dancing, then,' she teased. 'You're not going to teach me the flamenco.' She was leaning against the wall and putting on her ballet pumps, hardly a provocative move, except it was to him.

'Impressed with my Spanish, were you?'

'No Flamenco Medico?' She pouted and raised her arm and gave a stamp of her foot. Dominic stood there, his black eyes watching and sudden tension in his throat.

'Any chance of a drink?'

'Sure!' She beamed and headed to the kitchen and opened the fridge. 'I've got…' She stared at a jug of cordial, kicked herself for not grabbing some beer or wine, or olives and vermouth to make cocktails, she frantically thought.

'I meant water.'

'Oh, I think I've got some somewhere.' She grinned

and turned on the tap. 'Oh, yes, here it is.' Was that a reluctant smile on the edge of his lips? 'Here you go.' She
handed him the glass as his phone rang, and because
of his job he had no choice but to check it. Bridgette's
smile was a wry one as 'Arabella' flashed up on the
screen.

'She's hitting the bottle early tonight.'

He laughed. 'It's my birthday.'

'Oh!' It was all she could think of to say and then her
brain sort of slid back into functioning. 'Happy birthday,' she said. 'I've got candles but no cake.'

Then the phone rang again and they stood there.

And she was annoyed at his ex, annoyed that he was
standing there in her kitchen, and her eyes told him so.
'You really did break her heart, didn't you?'

'Long story,' he said. He didn't want to talk about it,
hadn't ever spoken about it, and really he'd rather not
now.

'Short version?'

'Come on,' he said, 'the table's booked.'

'You know what?' Bridgette said. 'I'm not very hungry.'

'You just said you were starving.'

'Not enough to sit through five hundred phone calls
from your ex.'

'Okay, okay.' He offered a major concession. 'I'll
turn it off.'

'No,' she said. 'I'm not doing it any more, putting
up with crap.' She was talking about Paul, but she was
talking about him too, or rather she was talking about

herself—she would not put herself through it again. 'Even if you turn it off, I'll know she's ringing. What's that saying? If a tree falls in a forest, does it make a noise?'

'What?' He was irritated, annoyed, but certainly not with her. 'I've said I'll turn it off, Bridgette. She doesn't usually ring—I never thought when I asked you to come out that it was my birthday. I don't get sentimental, I don't sit remembering last year, blah blah blah.'

'Blah blah blah…' Bridgette said, her voice rising, irritated and annoyed, and certainly it was with him. 'That's all she was, blah blah blah.' The night was over before it had even started. She really should have left it at one night with him. 'What is it with men?' She stormed past him, completely ready to show him the door, and it was almost a shout that halted her.

'She didn't want my brother and his friends at our engagement party.'

They both stood, in a sort of stunned silence, he for saying it, she that he had.

'He's got Down's,' Dominic said, and she was glad that she knew already. 'He lives in sheltered housing. When I'm there I go over every week and sometimes she came with me. She was great…or I thought she was, then when we were planning the engagement, my dad suggested it might be better if Chris didn't come, Chris and his friends, that we have a separate party for them, and she agreed. "It might be a bit awkward."' He put on a very plummy voice. '"You know, for the other guests. You know how he loves to dance."'

And Bridgette stood there and didn't know what to say.

'I couldn't get past it,' Dominic said, and he'd never discussed this with another person, but now that he'd started, it was as if he couldn't stop. Months of seething anger and hurt for his brother all tumbling out. 'My dad wanted nothing to do with him when he was born, he has nothing to do with him now, and it turned out Arabella didn't want him around either—well, not in the way I thought she would.'

'I'm sorry.' It was all she could say and she could hear the bitterness in his response.

'She keeps saying sorry too—that she didn't mean it and if we can just go back of course he can come to our party. She claims that she said what she did because she was just trying to get on with my dad, except I heard it and I know that it was meant.' He shook his head. 'You think you know someone...'

And when the phone rang again she decided that she did know what to say, after all.

'Give it to me,' she said, and she answered it and gave him a wink and a smile as she spoke. 'Sorry, Dominic's in bed...' She looked at him, saw him groan out a laugh as she answered Arabella's question. 'So what if it's early? I never said that he was asleep.' And she put down the phone but didn't turn it off. Instead she put her hand to her mouth and started kissing it, making breathy noises. Then she jumped up onto the bench, her bottom knocking over a glass.

'Dominic!' she shrieked.

'Bridgette!' He was folded over laughing as he turned off the phone. 'You're wicked.'

'I can be,' she said.

And he looked at her sitting on the bench all dishevelled and sexy, and thought of the noises she had made and what she had done, and just how far they had come since that night. Her words were like a red rag to a bull—he sort of charged her, right there in the kitchen.

Ferocious was his kiss as he pushed her further up the bench, and frantic was her response as she dragged herself back.

His hands were everywhere, but she was just as bad—tearing at his shirt till the buttons tore, pulling out his belt, and she was delighted that they weren't going to make it to the bedroom again, delighted by her own condom-carrying medico. Except Dominic had other ideas.

'Bed.' He pulled her from the bench. 'This time bed.'

'No.' She pulled at his zipper. 'No, no, no.'

'Yes.' He didn't want the floor again. He was leading her to her room, dragging her more like as she dug her heels in.

'You can't go in there!'

'Why?' He grinned, except he'd already pushed the door open. 'Have you got more babies stashed away that you haven't told…?' He just stopped. She doubted anyone as glamorous as he had seen a really messy bedroom, like a *really* messy one. He looked at the chaos and then at the beauty that had somehow emerged out of it.

'I told you not to go in there!' She thought she'd killed the moment. Honestly, she really thought she had, but something else shifted, something even more breathtaking than before.

'In here now, young lady.' His voice was stern as he pointed, and she licked her lips, she could hardly breathe for the excitement, as she headed to her bedroom. 'You can hardly see the bed,' he scolded as he led her to it. 'I've a good mind...'

Yes, they *were* bad. He did put her over his knee, but she nearly fell off laughing and they wanted each other too much to play games. It was the quickest sex ever, the best sex ever.

Again.

Again, she thought as he speared into her. They were still half-dressed, just mutual in want. She'd wanted him so badly again and now he was inside her.

It was bliss to have him back, to be back, to scream out as he shuddered into her.

Bliss for it already to have been the perfect night and it was only seven-thirty p.m.

To be honest, as she looked over he seemed a bit taken back by what had happened.

'Bridgette...' Please don't say sorry, she thought. 'I had no intention...' He looked at her stricken face. 'I mean...I had a table booked and everything.'

'You're not sorry, then?'

'Sorry?' He looked over to her. 'I couldn't be less sorry, just...' He might even be blushing. 'I did want to talk, to take you out. We could still go...'

'If you can sew on your own buttons!' Bridgette looked at his shirt. 'But first you'd have to find a needle. And thread,' she added after a moment's thought.

They settled for pizza. Bridgette undressed and slid into bed, and there would be time for talking later, for now they filled the gap and her roaring hunger with kissing until the pizza was delivered, and then he undressed and got into bed too.

And they did have that grown-up conversation. It sort of meandered around other conversations, but the new rules were spoken by both of them. It was difficult and awkward at times too, but so much easier naked in bed and eating than at some gorgeous restaurant with others around. They spoke about nothing at first and then about work.

'I don't get close.' Dominic shook his head. 'I'm good at my job. I don't need to be like some politician and hold and cuddle babies to be a good doctor.'

'Never?' she checked.

'Never,' Dominic said. 'Oh, I held little Esperanza, but that was more for the parents, for the *abuela*, but...' He *did* try to explain it. 'I said she was cute and, yes, she is, but they're not going to get a touchy-feely doctor if they are on my list.' He said it and he meant it. 'I can't do that. I know all that might happen—I can't get involved and then in a few weeks have to tell them that the news isn't good.' He was possibly the most honest person she had met. 'I'll give each patient and their parent or parents one hundred per cent of my medical mind. You don't have to be involved to have compassion.' It was too easy to be honest with her, but sometimes the truth hurt. 'I couldn't do it, Bridgette. I couldn't do this job if I got too close—so I stay back. It's why I don't want kids of my own.' He gave her a nudge. 'That's why I don't get involved with anyone who has kids.'

'I don't have kids.' Bridgette said. 'And I think it wasn't just the long-term viability of our future you were thinking about that night…' She nudged him and he grinned, though she didn't repeat midwife-speak to him; instead she spoke the truth. 'Here for a good time, not a long time…and not have the night interrupted with crying babies.'

'Something like that.'

'Didn't Arabella want kids?'

'God, no,' Dominic said.

The conversation sort of meandered around, but it led to the same thing.

They both knew it.

'I will be moving back to Sydney.' He was honest. 'It's not just work. It's family and friends.' And she nodded and took a lovely bite of cheesy dough and then without chewing took another. She couldn't blame him for wanting to be with them. She took another bite and he told her about his brother, that he'd been thirteen when Chris was born. 'To be honest, I was embarrassed—I was a right idiot then. So was my dad,' he said. 'They broke up when he was three. I was doing my final year school exams and all stressed and self-absorbed and Chris would just come in and want to talk and play—drove me crazy.

'He didn't care that I had my chemistry, couldn't give a stuff about everything that was so important to me—except clothes. Even now he likes to look good, does his hair.' Dominic grinned. 'Loves to dance!' He rolled his eyes. 'Loves women…'

'Must be your brother!' Bridgette smiled—a real one.

'When I was doing my exams I'd be totally self-centred, angry, stressed. "What's wrong, Dom?" he'd ask. And I'd tell him and he'd just look at me and then go and get me a drink or bring me something to eat, or try to make me laugh because he didn't get it. You know, I stopped being embarrassed and used to feel sorry for him. My dad didn't have anything to do with him, but then I realised Chris was the one who was happy and feeling sorry for me!'

'We've got it all back to front, you know,' Bridgette admitted.

'He's great. And you're right…' He saw her frown. 'I'm not like a paediatrician. I was like my dad growing up—just me, me, me. Without Chris I would have been a sports doctor on the tennis circuit or something—I would,' he said, and she was quite sure he was right, because he had that edge, that drive, that could take him anywhere. 'I'd certainly have had a smaller nose.'

'What?' She frowned and he grinned. 'My father thought I needed a small procedure. I was to have it in the summer break between school and university. He had it all planned out.' He gave a dark laugh. 'The night before the operation I rang him and told him to go jump.'

'Do you talk now?'

'Of course.' He looked over. 'About nothing, though. He never asks about Chris, never goes in and sees him on his birthday or Christmas, or goes out with him.' He gave her a grin. 'I can still feel him looking at my nose when he speaks to me.'

'He'd be wanting to liposuction litres out of me!' Bridgette laughed and he did too.

Dominic lay and stared up at the ceiling, thought about today—because even if he did his best not to get close to his patients, today he hadn't felt nothing as he'd stood and had that photo taken. He'd been angry—yes, he might have smiled for the camera, but inside a black anger had churned, an anger towards his father.

He'd walked up to NICU and Tony had walked along-side him, had stood with his baby for every test, had beamed so brightly when the good news was confirmed that her heart was fine.

'I'll come back to Maternity with you in case Maria has any questions,' Dominic had said, even though he hadn't had to. He had stood and watched when Tony told his wife the good news and wondered what he'd have been like had he had Tony as a father. He didn't want to think about his father now.

'How long have you been looking after Harry?' he asked instead.

Bridgette gave a tense shrug. 'It's very on and off,' she said.

'You said she was a lot younger...'

'Eighteen,' Bridgette said. He'd been so open and honest, yet she just couldn't bring herself to be so with him. 'I really would rather not talk about it tonight.'

'Fair enough,' Dominic said.

So they ate pizza instead and made love and hoped that things might look a little less complicated in the morning.

They didn't.

'Do you want to go out tonight?' he asked, taking a gulp of the tea she'd made because Bridgette had run out of coffee. 'Or come over?'

'I'd love to, but I truly can't,' she said, because she *couldn't*. 'I've got to pick Harry up.'

'When does his mum get back?'

'Tomorrow,' Bridgette said. 'I think.'

'You think.' Some things he could not ignore. 'Bridgette, you seem to be taking on an awful lot.'

'Well, she's my sister,' Bridgette said, 'and she's looking for flats and daycare. It's better that she has a few days to sort it out herself rather than dragging Harry around with her.'

'Fair enough.'

And he didn't run for the hills.

Instead he gave her a very nice kiss, and then reached in for another, a kiss that was so nice it made her want to cry.

'Have breakfast,' she said to his kiss, trying to think what was in the fridge.

And he was about to say no, that he had to go to work in an hour and all that.

Except he said yes.

He thought of the frothy latte he'd normally be sipping right now.

Instead he watched Bridgette's bottom wiggle as she made pancakes because she didn't have bread.

Watched as she shook some icing sugar over them.

How could you not have bread? she screamed inside.

Or bacon, or fresh tomatoes. She had thrown on her nursing apron—it had two straps with buttons and big pockets in the front. She had ten of them and they were brilliant for cooking—so the fat didn't splat—but she was naked beneath.

'We should be sitting at a table outside a café—' she smiled as he watched her '—or at the window, watching the barista froth our lovely coffees.'

She must have read his mind.

As she brought over two plates of pancakes, where Bridgette was concerned, he crossed the line. 'How long ago did you break up with Paul?'

'Excuse me?' She gave him a very odd look as she came over with breakfast. 'I don't remember discussing him with you.'

'You didn't.' He gave a half-shrug. 'You really don't discuss yourself with me at all, so I've had to resort to other means.' He saw the purse of her lips. 'I didn't just happen across it—I asked Vince for your e-mail address. Guys do talk.' He saw her raise her eyebrows.

'He said there had been a messy break-up, that was all he knew.'

'Well, it wasn't very messy for me.' Bridgette shrugged. 'It might have been a bit messy for him because he suddenly had to find somewhere to live.' She shook her head. She wasn't going there with him. 'It's a long story…'

'Short version,' Dominic said.

'We were together two years,' Bridgette said. 'Great for one of them, great till my sister got depressed and moved in and suddenly there was a baby with colic and…' She gave a tight shrug. 'You get the picture. Anyway, by the time Harry turned one we were over.' She had given the short version, but she did ponder just a little. 'He felt the place had been invaded, that I was never able to go out.' She looked over at him. 'Funny, I'd have understood if it had been his flat.' She gave Dominic a smile but it didn't reach her eyes. He could see the hurt deep in them and knew better than to push.

'I'll see you at work on Monday,' she said as she saw him to the door.

'I'm still here for a while,' Dominic said.

'And then you won't be…'

'It doesn't mean we can't have a nice time.' If it sounded selfish, it wasn't entirely. He wanted to take her out, wanted to know her some more, wanted to spoil her perhaps.

'Like a holiday romance?' Bridgette asked.

'Hardly. I'm working sixty-plus hours a week,' he said to soften his offering, because, yes, a brief romance was the most he could ever commit to. But she hadn't said it with sarcasm. Instead she smiled, because a holiday romance sounded more doable. She certainly wasn't about to let go of her heart and definitely not to a man like him. A holiday romance maybe she could handle.

'I won't always be able to come out... I mean...' Bridgette warned.

'Let's just see.' He kissed the tip of her nose. 'Who knows, maybe your sister will get that job, after all, and move up to Bendigo.'

And you should be very careful what you wish for, Dominic soon realised, because a few days later Courtney did.

CHAPTER EIGHT

AT FIRST it was great. Out had come the silver dress, and he *had* taught her the flamenco—not that he knew how, but they'd had fun working it out.

In fact, with Courtney and Harry away, it had been Dominic who had found himself the one with scheduling problems.

'I'll get back to you within the hour.' There was a small curse of frustration as Dominic put down the phone and pulled out his laptop.

'Problem?' Bridgette asked.

'Mark Evans wants me to cover him till eleven a.m. I'm supposed to be picking up Chris from the airport then.' He pulled the airline page up. Chris had been missing his brother, and with Dominic unable to get away for a while, a compromise had been reached and Chris was coming down to Melbourne for the night. 'I'd say no to Mark except he's done me a lot of favours. I'll see if I can change his flight.'

'You could just ask me,' Bridgette said, unable to see the problem. 'Surely if Chris can fly on his own, he won't mind being met by a friend of his brother's.'

'You sure?'

'It's no big deal.'

To Dominic it was a big deal. Arabella would, he re-alised, have simply had Chris change his flight, which was maybe a bit unfair on her, because Arabella would have been at work too. Bridgette was, after all, not start-ing till later. 'What if the flight's delayed? It doesn't leave you much time to get to your shift as it is...'

'Then I'll ring work and explain that I'm delayed. What?' She misread his curious expression. 'You don't think I'd just leave him stranded?'

Chris's flight wasn't delayed. In fact, it landed a full ten minutes early and he had hand luggage only, which left plenty of time for a drink and something to eat at an airport café before she started her late shift. He told her all about his first time flying alone and then they drove back to Dominic's, getting there just as he ar-rived. There was no denying that the two brothers were pleased to see each other. 'Come over tonight if you want,' Dominic said, 'after your shift. We're just see-ing an early movie so we could go out for something to eat if you like?'

'I'll give it a miss, thanks,' Bridgette said. 'I don't want to spoil your party and anyway I'm on an early shift tomorrow.' And he was always defensive around his brother yet not once did he think it was a snub. He knew Bridgette better than that—well, the part of Bridgette that she let him know. And he knew that she wouldn't even try to win points by hanging around to prove she was nothing like Arabella.

She *was* nothing like Arabella.

'See you, Chris.' She gave him a wave. 'Have a great night.'

'See you, Bridgette,' he said. 'Thanks for the cake.

'We went to a café,' Chris explained, when she had gone. 'Is that your girlfriend?'

'She's a friend,' Dominic said.

'Your girlfriend.' Chris grinned.

'Yeah, maybe,' Dominic admitted, 'but it's not as simple as that.' It wasn't and it was too hard to explain to himself let alone Chris.

There was a reason why holidays rarely lasted more than a few weeks—because any longer than that, you can't pretend there are no problems. You can't keep the real world on hold. Perhaps selfishly Dominic had wanted Courtney to leave, wanted to get to know a bit better the woman he had enjoyed dating, but once Chris had gone home, he realised that it wasn't the same Bridgette when Harry wasn't around. Over the next few days she couldn't get hold of Courtney and they were back to the morning after he'd met her—Bridgette constantly checking her phone. There was an anxiety to her that wasn't right.

He wanted the woman he'd found.

But Bridgette had that bright smile on, the one he had seen when they'd first met. She gave it to him the next Friday afternoon at work as she dropped off a new mum for a cuddle with her baby and he gave her his brief work nod back. Then she stopped by the incubator, as she often did, to speak with Carla.

'How are you?' she asked.

'Good today!' Carla smiled. 'Though it all depends on how Francesca is as to how I'm feeling at any moment, but today's been a good day. Do you want a peek?' There were drapes over the incubator and when she peeled them back Bridgette was thrilled by the change in the baby. She was still tiny, but her face was visible now, with far fewer tubes. It had been a precarious journey, it still was, but Francesca was still there, fighting.

'She gave us a fright last week,' Carla said. 'They thought she might need surgery on the Friday, but she settled over the weekend. Every day's a blessing still. I'm getting to hold her now—it's fantastic. Frank and I are fighting to take turns for a cuddle.'

It was lovely to see Francesca doing so well, but Bridgette's mind was on other things as she walked back to the ward, and she didn't hear Dominic till he was at her side.

'Hi.' He fell into step beside her. Not exactly chatty, he never was at work, but today neither was she. 'How's your shift?'

'Long,' she admitted. 'Everything's really quiet— I'm waiting for a baby boom.' She smiled when she saw Mary walking towards them.

'We're missing that little man of yours,' Mary said. 'How is he doing?'

'He's fine,' Bridgette said, expecting Dominic to walk on when she stopped to talk to Mary, but instead he stood there with them. 'I am sorry to have given you such short notice.'

'Hardly your fault.' Mary gave her a smile. 'You'd be missing him too?'

Bridgette gave a nod. 'A bit,' she admitted, 'but they should be home soon for a visit.'

'That's good.' Mary bustled off and Bridgette stood, suddenly awkward.

'Have you heard from her?'

Bridgette shook her head. 'I tried to ring but couldn't get through—I think she's out of credit for her phone. Right.' She gave a tight smile. 'I'm going to head for home.'

'I should be finished soon,' Dominic said. 'And then I'm back here tomorrow for the weekend.' He gave her a wry grin. 'Some holiday romance.'

'We can go out tonight,' Bridgette offered. 'Or sleep.'

'Nope,' Dominic said, 'we can go out and then…' He gave her that nice private smile. 'Why don't you head over to mine?' he asked, because there were cafés a stone's throw away, unlike Bridgette's flat.

'Sure,' Bridgette said, because she couldn't face pizza again and the flat still hadn't been tidied. The cot was down, but stood taking up half the wall in her spare bedroom, which made it an obstacle course to get to the computer.

Next weekend she was off for four days and she *was* going to sort it.

* * *

Bridgette let herself into his flat, and wondered how someone who worked his ridiculous hours managed to keep the place so tidy. Yes, he'd told her he had someone who came in once a week, and she knew he did, but it wasn't just the cleaner, Bridgette knew. He was a tidy person, an ordered person.

Knew what he wanted, where his life was going.

She had a little snoop, to verify her findings. Yes, the dishes were done and stacked in the dishwasher; the lid was on the toothpaste and it was back in its little glass. She peered into the bedroom—okay, it wasn't exactly hospital corners, but the cover had been pulled back up. She wandered back to his lounge and over to his desk.

There was a pile of mail waiting for him, one a very thick envelope, from that exclusive hospital where he wanted to work, but it was too much to think about and she had a shower instead. Then she pulled on a black skirt with a pale grey top, because an awful lot of her clothes seemed to live here now. The outfit would look okay with ballet pumps or high heels—wherever the night might lead.

It was a holiday romance, Bridgette kept telling herself to make sense of it, and summer was coming to an end. The clock would change soon and in a couple of weeks it would be dark by now. She felt as if she were chasing the last fingers of the sun, just knew things were changing. Oh, she'd been blasé with Mary, didn't want to tell anyone what was in the bottom of her heart, that things were building, that at any mo-

ment now the phone would ring and it would all have
gone to pot.

'Sorry about that…' He came in through the door
much later than expected and gave her a very haphazard
kiss as he looked at his watch and picked up his mail.
He didn't want her to ask what the hold-up had been,
didn't want her to know the scare little Francesca had
given him just a short while before. He had twelve hours
off before a weekend on call and he needed every moment of it, but first… 'I've got to take a phone call.'

'No problem.'

'Hey,' Dominic said when his phone rang promptly
at seven-thirty. 'How are you?'

'Good,' Chris said, and got straight to the point.
'When are you coming back to Sydney?' Chris was
growing impatient. 'It's been ages since you were here.'

And Dominic took a deep breath and told him the
news he hadn't really had time to think about, let alone
share with Bridgette. 'I got a phone call today, an—' he
didn't want to say too much at this early stage '—I'm
coming home for a few days next weekend. We'll go
out then.'

'It's been ages.'

'I know,' Dominic said, and he knew how much his
brother missed him, but he tried to talk him around, to
move the conversation to other things. 'What are you
doing tonight?'

'A party,' Chris said, and normally he'd have given
him details as to who was going, the music that would

be played, what they were eating, but instead he had a question. 'Bridgette *is* your girlfriend, isn't she?'

And normally Dominic would have laughed, would have made Chris laugh with an answer like 'One of them', but instead he hesitated. 'Yes.'

And usually they would have chatted for a bit—until Chris's Friday night kicked off and he was called out to come and join the party, but instead Chris was far from happy and told Dominic that he had to go and then asked another question.

'When are you properly coming back?'

'I've told you—I'm coming back soon for a few days,' Dominic said.

It wasn't, from Chris's gruff farewell, a very good answer.

'Right.' He came out of his room and saw that Bridgette was writing a note. 'Finally… Let's go and get something to eat. I've still got the sound of babies crying ringing in my ears.'

'Actually—' she turned '—my sister just called.' Back on went that smile. 'Things didn't work out in Bendigo and she's back. She's a bit upset and she's asked if I can have Harry tonight. I called and asked my parents, but they're out.'

'Oh.' He tried to be logical. After all, apart from one time in the corridor he'd never even seen Harry, and if her sister was upset, well, she needed to go. And even if more children was the last thing he needed tonight, she really had helped out with Chris and, yes, he did want to see her. 'We can take him out with us.'

'It's nearly eight o'clock,' Bridgette said, though when Harry was with her sister his bedtime was erratic at best.

'It's the Spaniard in me,' Dominic said.

Courtney, Dominic thought as he sat in the passenger seat while Bridgette collected Harry, didn't look that upset. But he said nothing as Bridgette drove. They'd gone out in her car because of baby seats and things, but they drove along to the area near his house and parked. It was cool but still light as they walked. She felt more than a little awkward. Walking along, pushing a stroller on a Friday night with Dominic felt terribly strange.

They sat out in a nice pavement café. They were spoiled for choice, but settled for Spanish and ate tapas. It was a lovely evening, but it was cool, even for summer. For Bridgette it was made extra bearable by one of Dominic's black turtlenecks and a big gas heater blazing above them. It was nice to sit outside and Harry seemed content, especially as Bridgette fed him *crema catalana.* Dominic had suggested it, a sort of cold custard with a caramel top, and Harry was loving his first Spanish dessert, but the mood wasn't as relaxed as it usually was. Dominic was lovely to Harry, there was no question about that, but Bridgette knew this wasn't quite the night he'd had planned.

'So, what's Courtney upset about?' He finally broached the subject

'I didn't really ask.'

'Does she do this a lot?'

Bridgette shot him a glance. 'It's one night, Dominic. I'm sorry for the invasion.' She was brittle in her defence and he assumed she was comparing him with Paul. She changed the subject. 'Have you been to Spain?'

'We used to go there in the summer holidays,' Dominic said. 'Well, their winter,' he clarified, because in Australia summer meant Christmas time. 'My father had a lot of social things on at that time, you know, what with work, so Chris and I would stay with Abuela.'

'And your mum?' Bridgette asked.

Dominic gave her an old-fashioned look, then a wry grin. 'Nope, she stayed here, looking stunning next to Dad. And I spent a year there when I finished school. I still want to go back, maybe work there for a couple of years at some point. It's an amazing place.'

And there were two conversations going on, as she ate thick black olives and fried baby squid, and he dipped bread in the most delicious lime hummus, and Harry, full up on the custard, fell asleep.

'I'd better get him back.'

They walked back along the beach road, a crowded beach full of Friday night fun, except Dominic was pensive. He was trying to remember the world before Chris had come along and Bridgette was for once quiet too.

She drove him back to his place. Harry was still asleep, and she didn't want to wake him up by coming in. Dominic had to be at work tomorrow, so there was no way really he could stay at hers.

And they kissed in the car, but it was different this time.

'Not your usual Friday night,' she said. 'Home by ten, alone!'

He didn't argue—she was, after all, speaking the truth.

CHAPTER NINE

RATHER than change things, the situation brought what was already coming to a head.

Dominic didn't know how best to broach what was on his mind.

He was used to straight talking, but on this Tuesday morning, lying in bed with Bridgette warm and asleep beside him, he didn't know where to start. He'd been putting this discussion off for a couple of days now, which wasn't at all like him.

'Hey, Bridgette.' He turned and rolled into her, felt her sleepy body start to wake, and he was incredibly tempted to forget what had been on his mind a few seconds ago and to concentrate instead on what was on his mind now. 'When do you finish?'

'Mmm...?' She didn't want questions, didn't want to think about anything other than the delicious feel of Dominic behind her. She could feel his mouth nuzzling the back of her neck and she wanted to just sink into the sensations he so readily provided, to let him make love to her, but automatically she reached for the phone that was on her bedside drawer, checked there were no messages she had missed and frowned at how early it was—it wasn't even six a.m.

'It's not even six,' she grumbled, because they hadn't got to bed till one—an evening spent watching movies and eating chocolate, laughing and making love, because neither wanted to talk properly.

'I know that you're off next weekend, but when do you actually finish?'

'I've got a long weekend starting Thursday at three p.m. precisely.' She wriggled at the pleasurable thought. 'I'm not back till Wednesday when I start nights. Why?'

'Just thinking.'

Though he didn't want to think at the moment, it could surely wait for now, Dominic decided, because his hands were at her breasts, and how he loved them, and her stomach and her round bottom. She was the first woman he loved waking up with.

It was a strange admission for him, but he usually loathed chatter in the morning. Arabella had driven him mad then too.

'Do you want coffee?' Arabella would ask every morning.

It was just the most pointless question.

Okay, maybe not for a one-nighter, but two years on, had she really needed to start each day with the same?

He looked at Bridgette's back, at the millions of freckles, and she was the one woman who could make him smile even in her sleep. 'Do you want coffee?' he said to a dozing Bridgette.

'What do you think?' she mumbled, and then...

'What's so funny?' she asked as he laughed and his mouth met her neck.

'Nothing.'

'So what are you lying there thinking about?'

'Nothing.'

'Dominic?'

He hesitated for an interminable second, his lips hovering over her neck and his hand still on her breast. 'I've been invited for an informal interview.' He was back at her neck and kissing it deeply. 'Very informal. It's just a look around...'

'In Sydney?'

Her eyes that had been closed opened then. She'd sort of known this was coming. He'd always said he wanted to work there; they'd been seeing each other just a few short weeks and there had been that envelope she'd peeked at.

'Yep—there's a position coming up, but not till next year. It's all very tentative at this stage—they just want me to come and have a look around, a few introductions...'

'That's good.'

And that wasn't the hard bit.

They both knew it and they lay there in silence.

Like an injury that didn't hurt unless you applied pressure, they'd danced around this issue from day one, avoided it, but they couldn't keep doing that for ever.

'Come with me,' he said. 'We could have a nice weekend. You could use the break before you start nights.'

She didn't want to think about it.

Didn't want to think about him going to Sydney, and there was still something else to discuss. Bridgette knew that, and Dominic knew it too.

There was a conversation to be had but it was easier to turn around, to press her lips into his. 'Bridgette...' Dominic pulled back. 'It would be great.' He gave her a smile. 'I won't inflict my family on you.'

'What?' She tried to smile back. 'You'll put me in some fancy hotel?'

'We'll be staying at my flat,' Dominic said—and there it was, the fact that he owned a flat in Sydney but he was only renting here. He had a cleaner there, coming in weekly to take care of things while he was temporarily away. 'Bridgette, you've known from the start that was where I was going.'

'I know that.'

'It's only an hour's flight away.'

She nodded, because his words made sense, perfect sense—it was just a teeny flight, after all—but her life wasn't geared to hopping on planes.

'Look,' Dominic said, 'let's just have a weekend away. Let's not think about things for a while. I'll book flights. The interview will be a morning at most. I'll see Chris...'

And so badly she wanted to say yes, to say what the hell, and hop onto a plane, to swim in the ocean, shop and see the sights, to stay in the home of the man she adored, but... 'I can't.'

'You've got days off,' Dominic pointed out.

'I really need to sort out my flat.' She did. 'I've been putting it off for ages.'

'I know,' Dominic said. 'Look, why don't I come round a couple of nights in the week and help with those shelves?'

'You!' She actually laughed. 'Will you bring your drill?' She saw his tongue roll in his cheek. 'Bring your stud finder...' she said, and dug him in the ribs. He would be as hopeless as her, Dominic realised. After all, his dad had never been one for DIY—he wouldn't know how to change a washer. But it wasn't the shelves that were the real problem. Yes, it would be so much easier to talk about stud finders, to laugh and to roll into each other as they wanted to, but instead he asked her again.

'If I can't do it—' he had visions of her being knocked unconscious in the night by his handiwork '—then I will get someone in and those shelves will be put up on your return,' he said. 'But it really would be nice to go away.'

'I can't,' she said, because she simply could not bear to be so far away from Harry. Courtney's silence was worrying her and it couldn't be ignored; also, she couldn't bear to get any closer to Dominic. To open up her heart again—especially to a man who would soon be moving away.

'Look, I have to go back this weekend.'

'Go, then!' Bridgette said. 'I'm not stopping you. I'm just saying that I can't come.'

'You could!' he said. He could see the dominos all

lined up, so many times he'd halted them from falling, and he was halting them now, because when talking didn't work he tried to kiss sense into her. She could feel her breasts flatten against his chest and the heady male scent of him surrounding her, and she kissed him back ferociously. It was as close as they had come to a row: they were going to have a row in a moment and she truly didn't want one, knew that neither did he. This way was easier, this way was better, this simply had to happen, because somehow they both knew it was the last time.

He kissed her face and her ears, he pushed her knees apart and they were well past condoms now. He slid into her tight warmth, went to the only place she would come with him and she did. They both did.

It was a regretful orgasm, if there was such a thing, because it meant it was over. It meant they had to climb back out of the place where things were so simple.

'I think a weekend away would be great.' He tried again. He'd heard the first click of the dominos falling and still he was trying to halt them. 'I think we need to get away. Look, if you don't want to go to Sydney…' He didn't want to let down Chris, didn't want to reschedule the interview, but he didn't want things to end here. He wanted to give them a chance. 'We could drive. There's a few places I want to see along the coast…'

'I can't this weekend,' she said. 'I told you, I've got the flat to sort out. Courtney's still upset…'

'Well, when can you?' And he let them fall. 'I want to get away on my days off.' He really did—it had been a helluva weekend at work. He wanted to be as far away from the hospital as possible this next weekend, didn't want to be remotely available, because he knew that if they called, he'd go in. What was he thinking, driving to the coast when he had an interview, letting down Chris? For what? So that they could stay in and wait for her sister to ring?

'Look, I know you help out your sister…' He simply did not understand her. In so many things they were open, there were so many things they discussed, but really he knew so little about her. There was still a streak of hurt in her eyes, still a wall of silence around her. 'But surely you can have a weekend off.'

'Maybe I don't want one,' Bridgette said. 'Maybe I don't want to go up to Sydney and to see the life you'll soon be heading back to.'

'Bridgette…' He was trying to prolong things, not end them. 'I don't get you.'

'You're not supposed to, that's not what we're about.' It wasn't, she told herself. It was supposed to be just a few short weeks—a break, a romance, that was all. It was better over with now. 'Just go to Sydney,' Bridgette said. 'That's what you want, that's where you've always been heading. Don't try and blame us ending on Harry.'

'I'm not blaming Harry,' Dominic said, and he wasn't. 'I'll admit I was a bit fed up with his aunt on Friday.'

'Sorry to mess up your night.' She so wasn't going to do this again. 'God, you're just like—'

'Don't say it, Bridgette,' Dominic warned, 'because

I am nothing like him.' He'd heard a bit about her ex and wasn't about to be compared to Paul. 'I'll tell you one of the differences between him and me. I'd have had this sorted from the start. Your sister's using you, Bridgette.' He looked at her, all tousled and angry, and truly didn't know what this was about.

'Do you think I don't know that?'

'So why do you let her?' He gave an impatient shake of his head. 'Do you know, I think you hide behind Harry. He's your excuse not to go out, not to get away.' Bridgette was right, Sydney *was* where he'd always intended to be—that was his hospital of choice and he wasn't about to have his career dictated to by Courtney.

'I'm going for the interview. I'm flying out on Thursday night. I'll text you the flight times. We'll be back Sunday night.'

'Don't book a ticket for me,' Bridgette said. 'Because I can't go.'

'Yes, you can. And, yes, I am booking for you,' Dominic said. 'So you've plenty time to change your mind.'

He did book the tickets.

But he knew she wouldn't come.

CHAPTER TEN

'SORRY to call you down from NICU.' Rebecca, the acci-
dent and emergency registrar, looked up from the notes
she was writing. It was four a.m. on Tuesday morning.
It had been a long day for Dominic and a very long
night on call. After the interviews in Sydney and long
walks on the beach with Chris, his head felt as if it was
exploding, not that Rebecca could have guessed it. He
was his usual practical self. 'I'm trying to stall Mum
by saying we're waiting for an X-ray.'

'No problem. What do we know so far?'

'Well, the story is actually quite consistent—Mum
heard a bang and found him on the floor. He'd climbed
out if his cot, which fits the injury. She said that he was
crying by the time she went in to him. It was her reaction that was strange—complete panic, called an ambulance. She was hysterical when she arrived but she's
calmed down.'

'Are there any other injuries you can see?'

'A couple of small bruises, an ear infection, he's a bit
grubby and there's a bit of nappy rash,' Rebecca said,
'but he is a toddler, after all. Anyway, I'm just not happy

and I thought you should take a look.' She handed him the patient card and as Dominic noted the name, as his stomach seemed to twist in on itself, a young woman called from the cubicle.

'How much longer are we going to be waiting here?' She peered out and all Dominic could think was that if he had not recognised the name, it would never have entered his head that this woman was Bridgette's sister. She had straggly dyed blond hair and was much skinnier. Her features were sharper than Bridgette's and even if she wasn't shouting, she was such an angry young thing, so hostile in her actions, so on the edge, that she was, Dominic recognised in an instant, about to explode any moment. 'How much longer till he gets his X-ray or CT or whatever?'

'There's another doctor here to take a look at Harry,' Helga, the charge nurse, calmly answered. 'He'll be in with you shortly—it won't be long.'

'Well, can someone watch him while I get a coffee at least?' Courtney snapped. 'Why can't I take it in the cubicle?'

'You can't take a hot drink—' Helga started, but Dominic interrupted.

'Courtney, why don't you go and get a coffee? Someone will sit with your son while you take a little break.

'Is that okay?' He checked with Helga and she sent in a student nurse, but Rebecca was too sharp not to notice that he had known the name of the patient's mother. 'You know her?' She grimaced as Courtney flounced out, because this sort of thing was always supremely awkward.

'I know his aunt.' Dominic was sparse with his reply but Helga filled in for him.

'Bridgette. She's a midwife on Maternity. She's on her way. I called her a little while ago—Courtney was in a right panic when she arrived and she asked us to.'

'Okay.' Dominic tried not to think about Bridgette taking that phone call—he had to deal with this without emotion, had to step out and look at the bigger picture. 'I'm going to step aside.' He came to the only decision he could in such a situation. 'I'm going to ring Greg Andrews and ask him to take over the patient, but first I need to take a look at Harry and make sure that there's nothing medically urgent that needs to be dealt with.' His colleague might take a while. He did not engage in further small talk; he did not need to explain his involvement in the case. After all, he was stepping aside. Dominic walked into the cubicle where Harry lay resting in a cot with a student nurse by his side. Rebecca came in with him.

'Good morning, Harry.' He took off his jacket and hung it on the peg and proceeded to wash his hands and then made his way over to the young patient. He looked down into dark grey eyes that stared back at him and they reminded him of Bridgette's. He could see the hurt behind them and Dominic did not try to win a smile. 'I expect you're feeling pretty miserable? Well, I'm just going to take a look at you.' Gently he examined the toddler, looking in his ears for any signs of bleeding, and Harry let him, hardly even blinking as he shone the ophthalmoscope into the back of each eye, not even crying or flinching as Dominic gently examined the tender bruise. Through it all Harry didn't say a word. 'Has he spoken since he came here?' Dominic asked

'Not much—he's asked for a drink.' The curtains opened then and Helga walked in. Behind her was Bridgette, her face as white as chalk, but she smiled to Harry.

'Hey.' She stroked his little cheek. 'I hear you've been in the wars.' She spoke ever so gently to him, but her eyes were everywhere, lifting the blanket and checking him carefully, even undoing his nappy, and he saw her jaw tighten at the rash.

'How is he?'

'He just gave everyone a fright!' Helga said, but Bridgette's eyes went to Dominic's.

'Could I have a quick word, Bridgette?'

He stepped outside the cubicle and she joined him.

'He's filthy,' Bridgette said. She could feel tears rising up, felt as if she was choking, so angry was she with her sister. 'And he didn't have any rash when I saw him on Friday. I bought loads of cream that she took—'

'Bridgette,' he interrupted, 'I'm handing Harry's care over to a colleague. You will need to tell him all this. It's not appropriate that I'm involved. You understand that?' She gave a brief nod but her attention was diverted by the arrival of her sister, and he watched as Bridgette strode off and practically marched Courtney out towards the waiting room.

'I'll go.' Helga was more than used to confrontations such as this and called to the nurses' station over her shoulder as she followed the two sisters out. 'Just let Security know we might need them.'

And this was what Courtney had reduced her to, Bridgette thought, standing outside the hospital early in the morning, with security guards hovering. But Bridgette was too angry to keep quiet.

'He climbed out of his cot!' Courtney was immediately on the defensive the moment they were outside. 'I didn't know that he climbed. You should have told me.' Maybe it was a good idea that security guards were present because hearing Courtney try to blame her for this had Bridgette's blood boiling.

'He's never once climbed out of the cot when I've had him,' Bridgette answered hotly. 'Mind you, he was probably trying to get out and change his own nappy or make himself a drink, or give himself a wash. You lazy, selfish…' She stopped herself then because if she said any more, it would be way too much. She paused and Helga stepped in, took Courtney inside, and Bridgette stood there hugging her arms around herself tightly, mortified when Dominic came out.

'This has nothing to do with you,' Bridgette said, still angry. 'You've stepped aside.'

'You know I had to.'

She did know that.

'Is this why you couldn't get away?' Dominic asked, and she didn't answer, because a simple yes would have been a lie. 'Bridgette?'

'I don't want to talk about it.'

'You never do,' he pointed out, but now really wasn't the time. 'I know that it doesn't seem like it now,' Dominic said, 'but Harry being admitted might be the best thing that could have happened. Things might get sorted now.'

As an ambulance pulled up she gave a nod, even if she didn't believe it.

'Bridgette, I was actually going to come over and see you today,' Dominic said, and she knew what was coming. 'I didn't want you to hear it from anyone else—I've just given notice. I'm leaving on Saturday.' He chose not to tell her just how impossible the decision had been, but in the end it had surely been the right one—he wanted simple, straightforward, and Bridgette was anything but. He'd opened up to her more than he had with anyone, and yet he realised that, still, despite his question, he knew very little about her and even now she said nothing. 'Anyway, I thought I should tell you myself.'

'Sure.'

'I'd better get up to...' His voice stopped, his stomach tightened, as the ambulance door opened and he met Tony's frantic eyes.

CHAPTER ELEVEN

DOMINIC checked himself, because it should make no difference that it wasn't Esperanza on the stretcher. Instead it was Roman, their three-year-old, and he needed Dominic's help and concentration just as much as his little sister would have. 'Dr Mansfield's here...' Tony was talking reassuringly to his son, who was struggling hard to breathe as they moved him straight into the critical area. 'The doctor who looked after Esperanza. That's good news.'

'He did this last year...' Tony said as Dominic examined him, and Tony explained about his severe asthma. 'He does it a lot, but last year he ended up in Intensive Care.'

'Okay.' Dominic listened to his chest and knew that Roman would probably have to head to Intensive Care again this morning.

Roman took up all of Dominic's morning, but by lunchtime, when he'd spoken to the family and the frantic *abuela*, things were a little calmer.

'While he's still needing hourly nebulisers it's safer that he is here,' Dominic explained, but then it was easier to speak in Spanish, so that Abuela understood. He told them things were steadily improving and would continue to do so.

Tony rang Maria, who was of course frantic, and Dominic spoke to her too.

'You get a taxi home,' Tony said to Abuela, 'and Maria can come in between feeds.'

Writing up his drug sheets, Dominic listened for a moment as they worked out a vague plan of action, heard that Tony would ring his boss and take today off.

'You think he might go to the ward tomorrow?'

'Or this evening.' Dominic nodded.

'I'll stay with him tonight and if you can come in in the morning to be with Roman I can go to work tomorrow,' Tony said to his mother. She rattled the start of twenty questions at him, but Tony broke in.

'We'll deal with that if it happens.'

Dominic headed down to the children's ward. Bridgette wasn't around and neither was Courtney. An extra layer had been added to Harry's cot, in case he was, in fact, a climber, and it stood like a tall cage in the middle of the nursery. He walked in and took off his jacket, washed his hands and then turned round and looked straight into the waiting grey eyes of Harry, who wasn't his patient, he reminded himself.

Harry's head injury wasn't at all serious, but he had been moved up to the children's ward mid-morning. Bridgette knew it was more of a social admission. Maybe she had done rather too good a job of reassuring her parents that it wasn't serious when she rang them, because they didn't dash in. After all, her father had to have a filling that afternoon, so they said they would come in the evening and, with a weary sigh, her mother agreed, yes, they would stop by Bridgette's flat and bring a change of clothes, pyjamas and toiletries.

Bridgette took the opportunity to voice a few of her concerns about his speech delay with the doctor and he gave her a sort of blink when she spoke about Harry's fixation with bricks and that he didn't talk much.

'Has he had his hearing checked?'

'Er, no.'

'He's had a few ear infections, though,' Dr Andrews said, peering through his examination notes. 'We'll get his hearing tested and then he might need an ENT out-patient appointment.'

Later they were interviewed by a social worker, but by dinnertime Courtney had had enough. 'I'm ex-hausted,' she said. 'I was up all night with him. I think I'll go home and get some sleep.'

'We can put a bed up beside his cot,' a nurse offered.

'I'd never sleep with all the noise,' Courtney said, gave Harry a brief kiss and then she was gone, safe in the knowledge that Bridgette would stay the night. Dominic was on the ward when Bridgette's parents arrived, talking with the charge nurse. She saw him glance up when her mother asked to be shown where Harry was.

'Here, Mum,' Bridgette said as they made their way

over, all nervous smiles, slightly incredulous that their grandson was actually here.

'Here's the bits you wanted,' her mum said, handing over a bag.

Bridgette peered into the bag and flinched. 'Did you deliberately choose the ugliest pyjamas I own?' She grinned. 'I'd forgotten that I even had these!' They were orange flannelette, emblazoned with yellow flowers, and had been sent by her granny about five years ago.

'You're lucky I could find anything in *that* room!' Betty said. 'I could barely see the bed.'

Yes, she really must get organised, Bridgette remembered. Somehow she had not got around to it last weekend. She had either been worrying about Harry or mooching over Dominic. Well, Dominic was gone or going and Harry would be sorted, so she would get organised soon.

'So what is he in for?' Maurice asked. 'He looks fine.'

He certainly looked a whole lot better. He'd had a bath and hair wash and had a ton of cream on his bottom. There was just a very small bruise on his head.

'He didn't even need a stitch,' Betty said.

'You know why he's in, Mum.'

'For nappy rash!' Betty wasn't having it.

'Mum… He's getting his hearing tested tomorrow.' They were less than impressed. 'Aren't you going to ask where Courtney is?'

'Getting some well-deserved rest,' Betty hissed. 'She must have had the fright of her life last night.' They didn't stay very long. They fussed over Harry for half an hour or so and it was a very weary Bridgette who tried to get Harry off to sleep.

'How's he doing?' Dominic asked as she stood and rubbed Harry's back.

'Fine,' Bridgette said, and then conceded, as she really wasn't angry with him, 'he's doing great. We're going for a hearing test tomorrow. Dr Andrews said we should check out the basics.' Of course he said nothing. He was his 'at work' Dominic and so he didn't fill in the gaps. 'I thought he was autistic or something.' She gave a small shrug. 'Well, he might be. I mean, if he is, he is...'

'You nurses.'

'You'd be the same,' Bridgette said, 'if he was...' Except Harry wasn't his and he wasn't hers either and it was too hard to voice so she gave him the smile that said keep away.

She washed in the one shower available for parents, an ancient old thing at the edge of the parents' room, and pulled on the awful pyjamas her parents had brought and climbed into the roller bed at seven-thirty p.m., grateful that the lights were already down. But she found out that Courtney was right—it was far too noisy to sleep. When she was woken again by a nurse doing obs around ten and by a baby coughing in the next cot, she wandered down to the parents' room to get a drink and nearly jumped out of her skin to see Dominic sprawled out on a sofa.

He'd changed out of his suit, which was rare for him,

and was wearing scrubs, and looked, for once, almost scruffy—unshaven and the hair that fell so neatly wasn't falling at all neatly now.

'Good God.' He peeled open his eyes when she walked in.

'Don't you judge me by my pyjamas,' Bridgette said, heading over to the kitchenette. 'I was just thinking you weren't looking so hot yourself—what happened to that smooth-looking man I met?'

'You did.' Dominic rolled his eyes and sort of heaved himself up. He sat there and she handed him a coffee without asking if he wanted one. 'Thanks.' He looked over at her. 'Bridgette, why didn't you say you were worried about Harry?'

'And worry you too? I haven't been ignoring things. I reported my concerns a few months ago, but I think I might have made things worse. I thought she was on drugs, that that was why she was always disappearing, but they did a screen and she's not. He's always been well looked after. Even now, he's just missed a couple of baths.' It was so terribly hard to explain it. 'They lived with me for nearly nine months, right up till Harry's first birthday.' She missed the frown on Dominic's face. 'And it was me who got up at night, did most of the laundry and bathing and changing. I just somehow know that she isn't coping on her own. Which is why I drop everything when she needs help. I don't really want to test my theories as to what might happen to Harry…'

'You could have told me this.'

'Not really holiday-romance stuff.'

'You've not exactly given us a chance to be anything more.'

'It's not always men who don't want a relationship,' Bridgette said. 'I always knew you were going back to Sydney and that I would stay here. It suited me better to keep it as it was.

'How was your weekend?' she asked, frantically changing the subject. 'How was Chris?'

'Great,' Dominic said. 'It's his twenty-first birthday this weekend, so he's getting all ready for that. Gangster party!' He gave a wry smile. 'I'm flying back up for that.'

'Have fun!' She grinned and didn't add that she'd love to be his moll, and he didn't say that he'd love it if she could be, and then his phone rang.

He checked it but didn't answer and Bridgette stood there, her cheeks darkening as Arabella's image flashed up on the screen.

'Well…' She turned away, tipped her coffee down the sink.

'Bridgette…'

'It doesn't matter anyway.'

Except it did.

He had seen Arabella—she'd found out he was back for the weekend and had come around. He'd opened the door to her and had surprised himself with how little he'd felt.

It would be easier to have felt something, to have gone back to his perfect life and pretend he believed she hadn't meant what she'd said about Chris. Easier than what he was contemplating.

'Bridgette, she came over. We had a coffee.'

'I don't want to hear it.' She really didn't, but she was angry too. It had been the day from hell and was turning into the night from hell too. 'It's been less than a week...' She didn't understand how it was so easy for some people to get over things. She was still desperately trying to get over Paul: not him exactly, more what he had done. And in some arguments you said things that perhaps weren't true, but you said them anyway.

'You're all the bloody same!'

'Hey!' He would not take that. 'I told you, we had coffee.'

'Sure.'

'And I told you, don't ever compare me to him.' He was sick of being compared to a man he hadn't met, a man who had caused her nothing but pain. 'I told you I'd have had this sorted.'

'Sure you would have.'

And in some arguments you said things that perhaps were true, but should never be said. 'And,' Dominic added, regretting it the second he said it, 'I'd never have slept with your sister.'

Her face looked as if it had been dunked in a bucket of bleach, the colour just stripped out of it. 'And you look after her kid—' Dominic could hardly contain the fury he felt on her behalf '—after the way she treated you?'

'How?' She had never been so angry, ashamed that

he knew. 'Did Vince tell you? Did Jasmine tell him?'
She was mortified. 'Does the whole hospital know?'

'I know,' Dominic said, 'because most people talk
about their break-ups, most people share that bit at the
start, but instead you keep yourself closed. I worked it
out,' he explained. 'Courtney and Paul both happened
to move out around Harry's first birthday...'

'Just leave it.'

'Why?'

'Because...' she said. 'I kicked my sister out, which
meant I effectively kicked my nephew out, and look
what it's been like since then.'

'Bridgette—'

'No.' She did not want his comfort, neither did she
want his rationale, nor did she want to stand here and
explain to him the hurt. 'Are you going to stay here?
Tell me we should fight for Harry?' She just looked at
him and gave a mocking laugh. 'You don't want kids
of your own, let alone your girlfriend's nephew.' She
shook her head. 'Your holiday fling's nephew.'

And he didn't want it, Dominic realised, and did that
make him shallow? He did not want the drama that was
Courtney and he did not want a woman who simply refused to talk about what was clearly so important.

'I'm going back,' Bridgette said. 'You can take your
phone call now.'

And two minutes later he did.

She knew because she heard the buzz of his phone
as she stood in the corridor outside, trying to compose
herself enough to head out to the ward.

She heard his low voice through the wall and there was curious relief as she walked away.

She was as lousy at one-night stands as she was at holiday romances.

There was only one guy on her mind right now, and he stood in the cot, waiting patiently for her return.

'Hey, Harry.' She picked him up and gave him a cuddle, and as Dominic walked past she deliberately didn't look up; instead she concentrated on her nephew, pulling back the sheets and laying him down.

It felt far safer hiding behind him.

CHAPTER TWELVE

COURTNEY rang in the morning to see how Harry's night had been and said that she'd be in soon. Bridgette went with Harry for his hearing test and then surprisingly Raymond, the ENT consultant, came and saw him on the ward. 'Glue ear,' Raymond informed her. 'His hearing is significantly down in both ears, which would explain the speech delay. It can make them very miserable. We'll put him on the waiting list for grommets.' It might explain the temper tantrums too, Bridgette thought, kicking herself for overreaction.

By late afternoon, when Courtney still hadn't arrived and Harry was dozing, Bridgette slipped away and up to Maternity, even though she'd rung to explain things. Rita *was* nice and surprisingly understanding.

'We're having a family meeting tomorrow,' Bridgette explained. 'I really am sorry to let you down. I'll do nights just as soon as I can.'

'Don't be sorry—of course you can't work,' Rita said. 'You need to get this sorted.'

Though her family seemed convinced there was nothing to sort, and as Bridgette walked onto the ward, she could see Courtney sitting on the chair beside Harry, all smiles. She was playing the doting mother or 'mother of the year', as Jasmine would have said. Dominic was examining Harry's new neighbor, young Roman, and Bridgette stood and spoke to Tony for a moment. Harry, annoyed that Bridgette wasn't coming straight over, stood up, put up his leg and with two fat fists grabbed the cot, annoyed that with the barrier he couldn't get over it—he was indeed a climber, it was duly noted, not just by the nurses but by Courtney. And Bridgette wondered if she was going mad. Maybe there was nothing wrong with her sister's parenting and she, Bridgette, had been talking nonsense all along.

'Thanks so much for staying last night,' Courtney said. 'I was just completely exhausted. I'd been up all night with him teething. Mum said that that can give them the most terrible rash…and then when he climbed out, when I heard him fall…'

'No problem,' Bridgette said. 'ENT came down and saw him.'

'Yes, the nurse told me,' Courtney said, and rather pointedly unzipped her bag and took out her pyjamas. Brand-new ones, Bridgette noticed. Courtney was very good at cleaning up her act when required. 'You should get some rest, Bridgette.' Courtney looked up and her eyes held a challenge that Bridgette knew she simply couldn't win. 'You look exhausted. I'm sure I'll see you at the family meeting and you will have plenty to say about his nappy rash and that I put him to bed without washing him to Aunty Bridgette's satisfaction.'

Dominic saw Courtney's smirk after Bridgette had kissed Harry and left.

He spoke for a moment with Tony, told him he would see him tomorrow. And Dominic, a man who always stayed late, left early for once and met Bridgette at her car. It wouldn't start, because in her rush to get to see Harry last night, she'd left her lights on.

'Just leave me.' She was crying, furious, enraged, and did not want him to see.

'I'll give you a lift.'

'So I can sort out a flat battery tomorrow! So I can take a bus to the meeting.' She even laughed. 'They'll think I'm the one with the problem. She's in there all kisses and smiles and new pyjamas. She'll be taking him home this time tomorrow.'

'She'll blow herself out soon,' Dominic said.

'And it will start all over again.' She turned the key one last hopeless time and of course nothing happened.

'Come on,' Dominic said. 'I'll take you home.'

They drove for a while in silence. Dominic never carried tissues, but very graciously he gave her the little bit of silk he used to clean his sunglasses. With little other option, she took it.

'I do get it.'

'Sure!'

'No, I really do,' Dominic said. 'For three years after Chris was born it was row after row. My father wanted him gone—he never came out and said it, didn't have the guts, and I can tell you the day it changed, I can tell you the minute it changed.' He snapped his fingers as he drove. 'My mother told him to get out because Chris wasn't going anywhere. She told him if he stayed in *her* home then he followed her rules.' They were at the roundabout and she wanted him to indicate, wanted to go back to his place, but instead he drove straight on. 'She got her fire back.' He even grinned as he remembered his trophy-wife mother suddenly swearing and cursing in Spanish. He remembered the drama as she'd filled his father's suitcases and hurled them out, followed by his golf clubs, as she picked up Chris and walked back in. 'I really want you to listen, Bridgette. You need to think about what you want before you go into that meeting. You will need to sort out what you're prepared to offer or what you're prepared to accept, not for the next week or for the next month but maybe the next seventeen years—you need to do the best for yourself.'

'I'm trying my best.'

'Bridgette, you're not listening to me. My mum could have gone along with Dad—she could have had a far easier life if she hadn't been a single mum bringing up a special-needs child. Chris could have been slotted into a home. Instead he went to one when he was eighteen, to a sheltered home with friends, and my mother did it so that he'd have a life, a real one. She did not want him to have to start over in thirty years or so when she was gone. She thought out everything and that included looking out for herself. What I said was you have to do the best for you—you have to look out for yourself in this…'

Dominic gritted his teeth in frustration as he could see that she didn't understand what he meant and knew that he would have to make things clear. 'The best thing that could happen is that Courtney suddenly becomes responsible and gets well suddenly, becomes responsible and looks after Harry properly—and we both know that's not going to happen. Now, you can run yourself ragged chasing after Courtney, living your life ready to step in, or you can work out the life you want and what you're prepared to do.'

She still didn't get it.

'Bridgette, she could have another baby. She could be pregnant right now!' She closed her eyes. It was something she thought about late at night sometimes, that this could be ongoing, that there could be another Harry, or a little Harriet, or twins. 'Come away with me on Saturday,' he said. 'Come for the weekend, just to see...'

'What about Arabella?'

'What about her?' Dominic said. 'I told her last night the same thing I told her when we had coffee on Saturday. We're through. And I've told her that I'm blocking her from my phone.' He knew he was pushing it, but this time he said it. 'You could be my moll!'

'I've got other things to think about right now.'

'Yes,' he said as he pulled up at her door. 'You do.'

And she didn't ask him in, and neither did he expect her to, but he did pull her into his arms and kiss her.

'Don't...' She pulled her head back.

'It's a kiss.'

'A kiss that's going nowhere,' she said. 'I'm not very good at one-night stands, in case you didn't work it out. And I really think the holiday is over…'

'Why won't you let anyone in?'

'Because I can't stand being hurt again,' Bridgette admitted. 'And you and I…' She was honest. 'Well, it's going to hurt, whatever way you look at it.' And she did open up a bit, said what she'd thought all those days ago. 'My life's not exactly geared to hopping on planes.'

'You only need to hop on one,' Dominic said, and he was offering her the biggest out, an escape far more permanent than her flat.

'Think about it,' he said.

'I can't.'

'Just think about it,' Dominic said. 'Please.'

He wished her all the very best for the next day, then drove down the road and pulled out his phone.

'It's Wednesday,' Chris said. 'Why are you ringing me on a Wednesday?'

'I'm just ringing you,' Dominic said. 'It doesn't only have to be on a Friday.'

'It's about Bridgette?' Chris said, and Dominic couldn't help a wry grin that he was ringing his brother for advice. 'The one with the baby.'

'It's not her baby,' Dominic said, because he'd explained about Harry as they'd walked along the beach.

'But she loves him.'

'Yep.'

'Well, why can't they come and live here?'

'Because it's not going to happen,' Dominic said. 'His mum loves him too.'

'And you can't stay there because you're coming over on Saturday,' Chris reminded him. 'For my birthday.' He heard the silence. 'You said you would.'

'I did.'

'See you on Saturday,' Chris said.

And Dominic did know how Bridgette felt—he was quite sure of that, because he felt it then too, thought of his brother all dressed up with his friends and his disappointment if *he* wasn't there. He thought of Bridgette facing it alone.

'You are coming?' Chris pushed.

'You know I am,' Dominic said. 'I'll see you then.'

'Are you still going to ring me on Friday?' Chris said, because he loathed a change in routine.

'Of course.'

CHAPTER THIRTEEN

'Hi, Tony!' Dominic said the next morning. 'Hi, Roman.' He tried not to look at Harry, who was watching him from the next cot. He'd seen all the Joyce family head off to the conference room, Courtney marching in front, the parents, as Bridgette would say, joined at the hip, and an exhausted-looking Bridgette bringing up the rear.

'Is this your last morning?' Tony said, because it was common knowledge now that he was leaving.

'No,' Dominic said. 'I'm on call tonight.'

'Well, if I don't see you I just want to be sure to thank you for everything with Roman and Esperanza and Maria,' Tony said.

'You're very welcome,' Dominic said. 'How are they both doing?'

'They're amazing,' Tony replied. 'Maria's a bit torn of course. She wants to be here more, but she doesn't want to bring Esperanza here…'

'Better not to,' Dominic said. He finished examining Roman and told his father he was pleased with his progress and that hopefully by Monday Roman would be home.

'It will be nice to have a full house again,' Tony said. 'Thought we couldn't have children—three goes at IVF for the twins, then Roman surprises us and now Esperanza!'

Dominic carried on with his round and tried not to think what was going on in the conference room, tried not to think about the offer he had made last night.

Bridgette couldn't *not* think about it.

She had pondered it all night, had been thinking about it in the car park for the hour she had waited to sort out her battery, and she was feeling neither hopeful nor particularly patient with her family. She sat there and the meeting went backwards and forwards, like some endless round of table tennis, getting nowhere. She listened to Courtney making excuses and promises again, watched her parents, who so badly wanted to believe their youngest daughter's words. She listened to the social worker, who, Bridgette realised, was very willing for Harry's aunt to support her sister—and of course she didn't blame them; but she realised that no one was ever going to tell her that she was doing too much. She had to say it herself.

'This is what I'm prepared to do.' She looked around the room and then at her sister; she took over the bat and slammed out her serve and said it again, but a bit louder this time.

'This is what I'm prepared to do,' she repeated. And when she had the room's attention, she spoke. 'Harry is to attend daycare here at the hospital, whether he's staying with you or being babysat by me—there has to be some consistency in his life. I will pay for his place if that is a concern you have, but he has to be there Monday to Friday from now on.' She looked at the social worker. 'If I can get a place again.'

'I can sort that out.' She nodded. 'We have a couple of places reserved for special allocations.' Bridgette turned to her parents. 'Mum, if I'm on a late shift or working nights and Harry is in my care, for whatever reason, you have to collect him or stay overnight. I can't always work early shifts.'

'You know we do our best!' Betty said. 'Of course we'll pick him up.'

Bridgette looked over at the caseworker, who gave a bit of a nod that told her to go on. 'He's due to have surgery…' She was finding a voice and she knew what to do with it, was grateful for Dominic's advice because she'd heeded it. 'He's on the waiting list for grommets and if that comes up while he's in my care I want to be able to go ahead. I want written permission obtained so that when Harry is in my care, or at any time I'm concerned, I can speak to doctors and I can take him to appointments. And I want—'

'I don't want him in daycare,' Courtney chimed in. 'I've told you—I'm not going anywhere. I decide what treatment he has and who he sees.'

'That's fine.' Bridgette looked at her sister. 'You have every right to refuse what I'm offering. But I can't stand aside any more. If you don't accept my conditions…'

It was the hardest thing she would ever say and could only be said if it was meant. Whether he was serious or not, she was incredibly grateful for Dominic's offer last night. 'Then you can deal with it. I'll move to Sydney.'

'Bridgette!' Her mum almost stood up. 'You know you don't mean that.'

'But I do—because I can't live like this. I can't watch Harry being passed around like a parcel. So it's either you accept my terms or I'm moving to Sydney.'

'You said you'd always be there for me.' Courtney started to cry, only this time it didn't move Bridgette. 'You promised…'

'Well, that makes us both liars, then,' Bridgette said. 'Because I can remember you saying exactly the same to Harry the day he was born.'

'Bridgette.' Her mum was trying to be firm, to talk sense into her sensible daughter. 'You know you're not going anywhere. Why Sydney?'

'I've met someone,' Bridgette said. 'And he's from there.' Betty had seen the happy couple, that were back as Bridgette's screensaver, when she'd had a nose in her daughter's spare room, had tutted at the two faces smiling back, and she had a terrible feeling her daughter might actually mean what she was saying.

'You love Courtney…' Maurice broke in.

'I'm not sure if I do,' Bridgette said, and she truly wasn't sure that she did. 'I honestly don't know that I do.'

'You love Harry.' Betty triumphed.

'Yes, I do. So if she wants my help then she can have

it, but those are my conditions and she needs to know
that any time I think Harry is at risk I will speak up.'
She walked out of the meeting because she had nothing
left to say. It had to be up to Courtney. She walked over
to the ward and saw Harry sitting in his cot, building
his bricks. She let down the cot side and held out her
arms. She had meant every word she had said in that
room, had convinced herself of it last night, but there
was a piece of her that was hidden apart, a piece of her
that no one must ever see, because as she picked up her
nephew and buried her face in his curls, she knew she
could never leave him. They just had to believe that
she might.

Dominic watched her cuddling Harry and he wanted
to go over, to find out what was happening, but instead
he picked up the phone.

It was the longest morning, even though he had
plenty to do, but he could not get involved, or be seen
to be getting involved, which surely she knew, but still
he felt like a bastard.

'Do you want me to give Harry his lunch?' Jennifer,
one of the nurses, offered. 'You can go to the canteen,
maybe have a little break?'

'I'm fine,' Bridgette said. 'They're still in the meeting. I'll give him his lunch and then—' she took a deep
breath '—I'm going home.'

'Jennifer!' Dominic's voice barked across the ward.
'Can you hold on to Harry's lunch for now, please, and
keep him nil by mouth until I've spoken to his mum?'

'What's going on?' Bridgette frowned.

'I've no idea,' Jennifer admitted. 'Wait there and I'll find out.' And she went over and spoke to Dominic, but instead of coming back and informing Bridgette, Jennifer headed off to the conference room. The group was just coming out and it was clear that Courtney had been crying but, along with Jennifer, they all headed back inside.

'What's going on?' She went up to him.

'Someone's coming down to speak to his mother.'

'Dominic!' She couldn't believe he'd do this to her.

'I'd go home now if I were you.'

'You know I can't.'

'Yes,' he said. 'You can.' She looked at him, met those lovely black eyes and somehow she trusted him. 'Go home,' he said. 'I'm sure you've got an awful lot to do.' She just stood there. 'Maybe tidy that bedroom, young lady.'

And she trusted him, she really did, but she knew he was leaving tomorrow, knew that right now he was saying goodbye.

'Go,' he said, 'and when she calls, don't come back.' He gave her a small wink. 'You only answer if it's me.'

'I can't do that. I can't just leave him.'

'You can,' he said. 'I'm here.'

CHAPTER FOURTEEN

WHEN her phone rang fifteen minutes later, she was driving, just approaching the roundabout, and she didn't pull over so she could take the call, as she usually would have. She didn't indicate when she saw that it was Courtney and instead she drove straight on.

Dominic was there.

She felt as if Dominic was there in the car beside her.

It rang again and this time it was her mum. Still, she ignored it.

Then it rang again as she arrived home and she sat at her computer before answering.

'Oh. Hi, Mum!'

'You didn't pick up.'

'I was driving.'

'Where are you?' she asked. 'I thought you'd gone down to the canteen.'

'I'm at home,' she said, as if she was breathing normally, as if home was the natural place she should be.

'Well, you need to get here!' Bridgette stared at her screensaver and tried to shut out the sound of her mother's panic. 'The doctors are here and they say

Harry needs an operation. There's a space that's opened up on the list and they want him to have an operation!' she said again really loudly.

'What operation?'

'He has to have surgery on his ears, and if she doesn't sign the consent, he'll go back on the list...' She could hear the panic in her mother's voice. 'Bridgette, you need to get here. You know what your sister's like—Courtney can't make a decision. She's gone off!'

'It's a tiny operation, Mum. It could do him an awful lot of good.'

'Bridgette, please, they've added him to the list this evening. Courtney's going crazy!'

'Mum...' Bridgette looked into Dominic's eyes as she spoke, and then into her own and wanted to be her again, wanted to be the woman who smiled and laughed and lived. 'It's up to Courtney to give consent. If not, he can go on the waiting list and wait, but it would be a shame, because his hearing is really bad.' She stood up. 'I've got to go, Mum. I've got things to do. Give Harry a big kiss from his aunty Bridgette. Tell him that I'll bring him in a nice present for being brave.' And she rang off.

She took the phone into the bathroom with her and because she didn't have any bubble bath, she used shampoo, put on a load of washing while she was waiting for the bath to fill and every time the phone rang, she did not pick up.

And then she did her hair, straightened it and put on blusher and lipstick too, even though she knew Dominic was on call and wouldn't be coming round. Then when her phone finally fell silent, she tackled her bedroom, worked out how to use a stud finder and put up the shelves that had been sitting in cardboard for way too long. Then the phone bleeped a text and it was from Dominic.

She took a breath and read it.

Op went well—he's back on ward and having a drink. Home tomoz.

She felt the tension seep out of her.

Should I come in now?

She was quite sure what the response would be, that he'd tell her to stay put, that Courtney was there and to let her deal with it, but as she waited for his reply, there was a knock at the door and when her phone bleeped he didn't say what she'd thought he might.

No, stay put—your mum's with him.

She wanted to know what was happening so badly. She had this stupid vision it was him as, phone in hand, she opened the door.

Instead it was her father and Courtney.

CHAPTER FIFTEEN

IT WAS a long night and he was glad when it hit six a.m. and there were just a couple of hours to go.

'Cot Four.' Karan, the night nurse, looked up from the baby she was feeding. 'I'll be there in a minute.'

'I'll be fine,' Dominic said, and headed in.

He took off his jacket, glanced again at Harry, who sitting there staring, and then proceeded to wash his hands. When he turned around, Harry was smiling. Dominic couldn't help himself from looking at the pull-out bed beside him, relieved to see that Betty was there.

He didn't know what had happened.

He'd heard the explosions from the fuse he'd lit when he'd asked for a favour from Raymond and a certain blue-eyed theatre nurse, but he'd been up and down between here and NICU and had never caught up as to what had really gone on.

He smiled back at Harry and then headed over to the cot opposite him, carefully examining the baby who was causing concern, pleased with her progress.

'How's Harry Joyce?' he asked Karan. He had every right to enquire as he was the paediatrician on call that night and Karan wouldn't know that he had stepped aside from the case.

'He's doing well.' Karan smiled. 'You could see the difference in him almost as soon as he came back from Theatre. He must have been struggling with his ears for a while. He's much more smiley and he's making a few more noises, even had a little dance in his cot. He's off home in the morning to the care of Mum.' She pulled out a notebook. 'Hold on a moment. Sorry, he's home with his aunt tomorrow. There was a big case meeting today apparently. Lots of drama.' She rolled her eyes. 'I haven't had a chance to read the notes yet.' She stood up and collected the folder and put it in front of him. 'Should make interesting reading.'

Karan walked back to the nursery to put down the baby she had been feeding and Dominic sat there, tempted to read the notes, to find out all that had gone on. It would be so easy to. 'So this is your last morning.' Tony stopped by the desk, just as Dominic went to open the folder. Tony had been up and used the parent showers before all the others did, was dressed and ready for when Abuela came in.

'It is,' Dominic said. 'I'm flying to Sydney this afternoon.'

'Well, thanks again.' Tony stifled a yawn.

'You must be exhausted.' It was Dominic who extended the conversation.

'Ah, but it's Saturday,' Tony said. 'I'm going home to sleep. That's if the twins and Esperanza let me.'

'You've got a lot on your plate,' Dominic said, but Tony just grinned.

'Better than an empty plate.'

Dominic stood up and shook Tony's hand and when Tony had gone he stepped away from the notes. Bridgette didn't deserve her ex reading up on her private life. If he wanted to know, he should ask her.

CHAPTER SIXTEEN

'HARRY!' She took him into her arms and wrapped him in a hug, truly delighted to have him home. 'I've got a surprise for you.' And she carried him in to what had been her study as well as Courtney's room and spare room. The cot had been folded and put away (well, it had been neatly put away under Bridgette's bed till she hauled it to the charity shop on Monday) and the bed that had been under a pile of ironing now had a little safety rail, new bedding and a child's bedside light. There were new curtains, a new stash of bricks in a toy box and an intercom was all set up.

'You've been busy,' her mum said when she saw Harry's new bedroom. 'Isn't he a bit young for a bed?'

'Well, at least he can't climb out of it. I'll just have to make sure I close the bedroom door or he'll be roaming the place at night.'

'It looks lovely.' Betty smiled at her daughter. 'I'm sorry that we haven't been much help.'

'You have been,' Bridgette said, because she couldn't stand her parents' guilt and they had probably been doing their best.

'No,' her mum corrected. 'We've been very busy burying our heads in the sand, trying to pretend that everything was okay, when clearly it wasn't. We're going to be around for you much more, and Harry too.'

'And Courtney?' Bridgette watched her mother's lips purse. 'She needs your support more than anyone.'

'We're paying for rehab,' Betty said.

'It's not going to be an instant fix,' Bridgette said, but she didn't go on. She could see how tired her parents looked, not from recent days but from recent years. 'We can get through this, Mum,' Bridgette said, 'if we all help each other.'

'What about you, though?' It was the first time her father had really spoken since they'd arrived. 'What about that young man of yours, the one in Sydney?'

'Let's not talk about that, Dad.' It hurt too much to explore at the moment. It was something she wanted to examine and think about in private—when she had calmed down fully, when she was safely alone, then she would deal with all she had lost for her sister, again. But her father was finally stepping up, as she had asked him to, and not burying his head in the sand as he usually did—which was a good thing, though perhaps not right now.

'We need to discuss it, Bridgette.' He sat down and looked her square in the eye. 'We didn't know you were serious about someone.'

'It never really got a chance to be serious,' Bridgette said.

'We should have had Harry more.'

Yes, you bloody should have, she wanted to say, but that wasn't fair on them, because really it wasn't so much Harry who had got in the way; it had been her too—she hadn't wanted a relationship, hadn't wanted to let another close. 'Things will be different now,' Bridgette said instead.

'You could go away for the odd weekend now and then...' her dad said. And teeny little wisps of hope seemed to rise in her stomach, but she doused them—it was simply too late.

After her parents had gone, Bridgette made Harry some lunch and then cuddled him on the sofa. She did exactly what she'd tried not to—she let herself love him. Of course she always had, but now she didn't hold back. She kissed his lovely curls and then smiled into his sleepy eyes and told him that everything was going to be okay, that Mum was getting well, that she would always be here for him.

And she would be.

It was a relief to acknowledge it, to step back from the conflict and ignore the push and pull as to who was wrong and who was right—she wasn't young, free and single, she had a very young heart to take care of.

'You wait there,' she said to Harry as the doorbell rang. They were curled up, watching a DVD. Harry was nearly ready to be put down for his afternoon nap and Bridgette was rather thinking that she might just have one too.

'Dominic!' He was the last person she was expecting to see, though maybe not. She knew that he did care about her, knew he would want to know how she was.

He wasn't a bastard unfortunately. It would be so much easier to paint him as one—they just had different lives, that was all.

'I thought you had a gangster party to be at!'

'I've got a couple of hours till the plane.' He was dressed in a black suit. 'I've just got to put on a tie and glasses—Mum's sent me a fake gun, though I'd better not risk it on the plane.' His smile faded a touch. 'I wanted to see how the meeting had gone...'

'Didn't you hear?' Bridgette said, quite sure the whole hospital must have heard by now. 'Or you could have read the notes.' He saw her tight smile, knew that Bridgette, more than anyone, would have hated things being played out on such a public stage—it was her workplace, after all. She opened the door. 'Come in.'

He was surprised to see how well she looked, or perhaps *surprised* wasn't the right word—he was in awe. Her hair swished behind her as she walked, all glossy and shiny as it had been that first night, and he could smell her perfume. She looked bright and breezy and not what he had expected.

Back perhaps to the woman he had met.

'I didn't want to read the notes,' Dominic said, walking through to the lounge. 'Though I heard that Harry had come home with you...' His voice trailed off as he saw Harry lying on the lounge, staring warily at him. 'Hi, there, Harry.'

Harry just stared.

'What happened to the nice smile that you used to give me when I came on the ward?' Dominic asked, but Harry did not react.

'Do you want a drink?' Bridgette offered, though perhaps it was more for herself. She wanted a moment or two in the kitchen alone, just to gather her thoughts before they had to do what she had been dreading since the night they had first met—officially say goodbye. 'Or some lunch perhaps?' She looked at the clock. 'A late lunch.'

'I won't have anything,' Dominic said. 'I'll have something on the plane and there will be loads to eat tonight. A coffee would be great, though.' It had already been a very long day. 'You've changed the living room.'

'I've given Harry his own bedroom,' Bridgette said, 'and I quite like the idea of having a desk in here.' And she could breathe as his eyes scanned the room, be-cause, yes, she'd changed the screensaver again. Now it was a photo of Harry and his mum, a nice photo, so that Harry could see Courtney often.

'It looks nice,' he said as Bridgette headed out to the kitchen and Dominic stood, more than a little awk-ward, nervous by what he had to say. He wasn't used to nerves in the least—he always had a level head. He said what was needed and rarely any more. He took off his jacket and looked for somewhere to hang it, settling on the back of Bridgette's study chair. Turning around he saw Harry smile, half-asleep, lying on the sofa. He gave Dominic the biggest grin and then closed his eyes.

'What are you smiling at?' Bridgette asked Dominic

as she walked back in the room carrying two mugs and saw him standing there grinning.

'Harry,' Dominic answered, still smiling. 'That nephew of yours really does love routine.' He saw a little flutter of panic dart across her eyes, realised that she thought perhaps he was there to tell her something. He understood she had an overactive imagination where Harry was concerned. 'He smiles when I take my jacket off. I've just realised that now. Whenever I came onto the ward at night he watched me and frowned and then suddenly he gave me a smile. I could never work out why.'

'It's what you do.' Bridgette grinned, because she'd noticed it too. 'Before you wash your hands. I don't think I've ever seen you examine a patient with your jacket on. Funny that Harry noticed,' she mused. 'I guess when your world's chaotic you look for routine in any place you can find it.'

'Well, it doesn't look very chaotic to me. You've done great,' Dominic said. He waited while she put Harry down for his very first nap in his big-boy bed—Bridgette surprised that he didn't protest, just curled up and went straight to sleep. She gently closed the door. 'So,' he asked when she came back in, 'how did the meeting go?'

'You really didn't read the notes?' She was a little bit embarrassed and awkward that he might be here to question her *plans* to follow him to Sydney, because even though she hadn't given his name, if Dominic had read the notes, the indication would be clear. 'Because I was just bluffing...'

'Bluffing?' Dominic frowned. 'About what?'

'Getting a life.' Bridgette gave a wry smile. 'Moving to Sydney.'

'You said that at the meeting?'

'Oh, I said that and a whole lot more,' Bridgette admitted. 'I did what you suggested. I spent the time before the meeting trying to work out rules I could live with. I said that he had to attend daycare, but I had to be able to take him to a doctor if needed and to take him for any procedures if Courtney wasn't available. I said that Mum and Dad had to help more if Courtney wasn't around...that I was through looking out for Courtney, that I was only on Harry side.'

'You said all that?' He put down his coffee and took her hand. 'Well done. How did Courtney take it?'

'I didn't stay to find out,' she said. 'I just left the meeting. I hope you don't mind, but I said that I'd been seeing someone, that he lived in Sydney—it just made it seem more real to them. It made them believe that I would leave if I told them I had somebody who wanted me to go with them.'

'You did.'

And she'd no doubt cry about it later—but not now. 'Thank you,' she said. 'For getting him squeezed onto the list.' He gave a frown. 'I know you must have...'

'Well, I thought it might buy another night before she dropped her act, and when you came out of the meeting...' He looked at her, didn't want to tell her how hard it had been to step aside, to not be in that room, not as a doctor but sitting beside her. 'I figured she might drop it a little quicker if you weren't there to sort it out for her.'

'Well, it worked. She fell apart when she had to actually make a decision and it all came out. It isn't drugs—it's alcohol. She's just been slowly falling apart since I kicked her out.'

'It would have happened wherever she was,' Dominic said. 'It was probably going on here...'

And she nodded because, yes, it had been a bit.

And she thought of Harry's birthday that should have been about cordial and cake but instead her sister had chosen to party on—and so too had Paul.

'I hate what she did,' Bridgette said. 'I just couldn't have her stay after that.'

'Of course you couldn't.' Dominic thought for a moment, knew he had to be very careful with what he said. Certainly he was less than impressed with Courtney, but even if people didn't like it at times, he was always honest. 'But I think it's something you have to move on from. She's clearly made a lot of mistakes, but if you're going to be angry with anyone—' he looked at Bridgette, who so deserved to be angry '—then I think it should be with him.'

'It was both of them.'

'He took advantage.'

'Oh, and you never have—' She didn't get to finish.

'Never,' Dominic said. 'Not once. My sexual résumé might not be impressive to you, but...' He shook his head. 'Nope, what he did was wrong, and however awful your sister has been, I bet she's been trying to douse an awful lot of guilt about her treatment of you.'

Bridgette nodded. 'She's gone to rehab. It's three months and Mum and Dad are paying. She came over last night with Dad and said she was terrified of letting everybody down…which she may well do, so I'm not getting my hopes up, but I've made a decision to be here for Harry.' She saw him glance at his watch.

'Sorry, I'm rattling on…'

'It's not that. I have to leave in an hour. I can't miss that plane.' He took a deep breath. Really, he was finding this incredibly difficult—she seemed fine, better than fine, as if she wasn't missing him at all.

Wouldn't miss him.

But he would miss her.

Which forced him to speak on.

'What you said about Sydney, about having someone who wanted you there, you weren't exaggerating, Bridgette.' He took her hand and her fingers curled around his. Inside her, those little wisps of hope uncurled too, and it was so wonderful to see him, to have him sitting beside her, to know this was hard for him. 'I want this to work too. I just can't not be there for Chris,' he said.

'I was very unfair to you—it was ridiculous that I couldn't even get away for a single weekend, and it is about to change. I spoke to my parents this morning so maybe I can get away now and then, maybe I could come up on days off, or some of them.' She stared at her fingers being squeezed by his, and she wished he would jump in, would say that was what he wanted, but he let her speak on. 'And who knows what might happen in the future? Courtney might get well—'

'You're not going to leave Harry,' Dominic cut in. 'You might be able to convince them, but you'll never convince me. You're not going anywhere while Harry's so little.'

'No.' She could feel tears trickling down at the back of her throat and nose. She'd been so determined not to cry, to do this with dignity, to let him go with grace. She could see the second hand on his watch rapidly moving around, gobbling up the little time that they had left. 'No, I'm not going anywhere. Well, not long term.'

'And I don't think the odd weekend is going to suffice.'

'No,' she said, because it wouldn't be enough.

And they could talk in the time they had left, but what was the point? Bridgette realised there was no solution to be had, so instead of tears she gave him a smile, not a false one, a real one. And she put herself first for once, was completely selfish and utterly indulgent and just a little bit wild, because as he went to speak she interrupted him.

'Have we got time for a quickie before you go?'

'We need to talk,' Dominic pointed out.

'I don't need anything,' she cut in. 'I know what I want, though.'

And he wasn't going to argue with that.

He didn't know what he had expected to find when

he came over, how he'd expected her to be when he'd knocked at the door, but as always she'd amazed him. Then, as she opened the bedroom door, she amazed him all over again.

'Wow.' As he walked into her bedroom he let out a low whistle. 'You've got a carpet!'

'I know!'

'I'm impressed.' He looked at the shelves and politely didn't comment about five holes she had made in the wall—because he wouldn't know how to find a stud either.

'Just you wait.' She was at his shirt as she spoke. He pulled off her T-shirt and undid her bra and it slowed things down undressing each other, so they stripped off for themselves and then Bridgette peeled back the duvet.

'You get first feel…'

'Of what?' he asked, hands roaming her body, but she peeled off his hands and placed them on the bedding.

'Of my million-thread-count sheets. I was saving them for best…'

Which he was, Bridgette knew that, because he lay on the sheets and wriggled around and made appreciative noises, and then he pulled her in and kissed her.

'I want to feel them now,' she said.

So she lay on the sheets and wriggled around and made appreciative noises too.

And then he kissed her again.

'Don't let me fall asleep after,' Dominic said.

'After what?' She frowned, naked in his arms. 'If you really think you can just come here and have sex…'

She made him laugh and she loved making him laugh. She loved the Dominic others so rarely saw. When it was just the two or them, the austere, remote man seemed to leave—and he understood her humour and matched it. He made her laugh too, turned those cold black eyes into puppy-dog ones. 'I don't want sex, Bridgette. I just want to hold you.'

'Oh, no.' They were laughing so much they would wake up Harry.

'I just want to lie next to you…' he crooned.

'No.'

He straddled her.

'I just want to talk,' he said.

'No talking,' she begged.

It was a whole new realm for Dominic, like swimming in the ocean after a lifetime doing laps in a pool.

He did not know that you could laugh so much on a Saturday afternoon, that she could laugh even now as she lost him.

As she loved him.

It was a different kiss from any they had tasted before, a different feeling from any they had ever felt.

He kissed her slowly and more tenderly and *he* let himself love her—smothered her, physically, mentally, buried her and pressed her against her very best sheets. He wrapped his arms under her and drove into her till she wanted to scream, and she pressed her mouth to his chest and held on for dear life. She didn't know what the future held and she couldn't control it anyway, so she lived in the moment, and what a lovely moment it was. And she could cry afterwards and not be embarrassed or sorry.

It was a wonderful afternoon, and nothing like the one he had intended, the most delicious surprise. His head was spinning that she could love him like that when she considered it over between them.

'I've made some decisions too.' He took a deep breath, dived out of the pool and into the ocean, where it was rough and choppy but exhilarating and wild. 'When I went to resign this week, when I told them I wouldn't be back, I was offered a job.' He looked at her grey eyes that were for the first time today wary. 'Here.'

She felt little wisps of hope rising again, then she moved to douse them. They were guilty wisps. Surely this was wrong.

'I'm going to ring on Monday and take it.'

'You want to work in Sydney, though. Your family's there, your friends, Chris. You always wanted to work there. It's your goal.'

'Goals change,' Dominic said.

'What about your brother?'

'I'm not going to say anything to him yet,' Dominic said. 'It's his birthday.'

He shook his head, because he couldn't do it to Chris this weekend. 'Look, the job doesn't start for a month and I'm taking the time off. I'm not working. You and I will spend some proper time together, do some of that talking you so readily avoid, and we'll see how I go with Harry...'

'You could have told me!'

'I tried,' Dominic said. 'You didn't want to discuss it—remember? I'll be back on Monday and we can talk properly then.' He looked at his watch. 'I'm going to have to get going soon. This is one plane I can't miss.'

She lay in bed and stared up at the ceiling, tried to take in what he was saying. A month...

A month to get to know Harry, to see how they went, and then... She was happy, happier than she had ever felt possible, but it felt like a test. Then he turned around and maybe she should compromise too.

'I could ask Mum and Dad to come over.' She was torn. 'If you want me to come tonight...'

'I think Harry needs a couple of nights in his new bed, don't you?'

And she was so glad that he understood.

'I have to get back.' He smiled. 'Would it wake Harry if I had a shower?'

'Don't worry about that.' And she had a moment of panic, because Harry was being golden and sleeping now, but what about at two a.m. when he decided to wake up, what about when it was six p.m. and her mother hadn't picked him up from crèche? How would Dominic deal with those situations? She wasn't sure she was ready for this, not convinced she was up to exposing her heart just to have Dominic change his mind. 'I'll get you some towels.'

'Could you pass my trousers?' he asked as she

climbed out of bed. 'Oh, and can you get out my phone?' He snapped his fingers as she trawled through his pockets, which was something Bridgette decided they would work on. Sexy Spaniard he may be, and in a rush for his brother's party perhaps, but she didn't answer to finger snaps. 'I can't find it and don't snap your fingers again,' she warned him. 'Hold on, here it is.' Except it wasn't his phone. Instead she pulled out a little black box.

'That's what I meant.' He grinned. 'So, aren't you going to open it?'

Bridgette was honestly confused. She opened the box and there was a ring. A ring that looked as if they were talking about a whole lot more than a month.

'I thought we were going to take some time...'

'We are,' Dominic said. 'To get to know all the stuff and to work things out, but, compatible or not, there's no arguing from me.' He pulled her over to the bed. 'I love you.' He looked at her and to this point he still didn't know. 'And I hope that you love me?'

She had to think for a moment, because she had held on so firmly to her heart that she hadn't allowed herself to go there. And now she did. She looked at the man who was certainly the only man who could have taken her to his home that first night. She really was lousy at one-night stands, because she knew deep down she had loved him even then.

'If I say it,' she said, 'you can't change your mind.'

'I won't.' That much he knew. She was funny and kind and terribly disorganised too—there was nothing he might have thought he needed on his list for the perfect wife, but she was everything that was now required.

'How do you know?' she asked.

'I'm not sure…' Dominic mused. 'Chemistry, I guess,' he said.

'And Chris?' she said as he pulled her back to bed and put his ring on her finger. She realised the magnitude of what he was giving up.

'He'll be fine.' Dominic had thought about it a lot and was sure, because of something Tony had said. He should have thanked Tony, not the other way around, for far better a full plate than an empty one. He didn't want to be like his father, hitting golf balls into the sky at weekends, a perfect girlfriend waiting at home, with not a single problem. 'I'll go up at least once a month and he can come here some weekends. If I'm working you might have to…' He looked at her and she nodded.

'Of course.'

'We'll get there,' he said. 'You're it and I know you'll do just fine without me, but better with me.' He looked at eyes that weren't so guarded, eyes that no longer reflected hurt, and it felt very nice to be with someone you knew, but not quite, someone you would happily spend a lifetime knowing some more. 'And I'm certainly better with you.'

'Hey!' There was a very loud shout from down the hall. 'Hey!' came the voice again.

'Oh, no.' Bridgette lay back on the pillow as Harry completely broke the moment. 'Those bloody grommets. It's as if he's suddenly found his voice.'

Harry had found his voice and he knew how to use it! 'Hey,' Harry shouted again from behind his closed door. It was a sort of mixture between 'Harry' and 'Hello' and 'Have you forgotten me?'

'I'll get him.' Bridgette peeled back the sheet, liking the big sparkle on her finger as she did so.

'If you say you love me, I'll go and get him,' Dominic said, and pulled on his trousers, deciding he had to be at least half-respectable as he walked in on the little guy.

'If you go and it doesn't make you change your mind—' Bridgette grinned, knowing what he would find '—I'll say it then.'

It was the longest walk of his life.

He'd just put a ring on a woman's finger. Shouldn't they be sipping champagne, booking a restaurant, hell, in some five-star hotel having sex, not getting up to a baby?

But with him and Bridgette it was all just a little bit back to front and he'd better get used to the idea.

He pushed open the door.

'Hey!' Angry eyes met him, and so did the smell. Angry eyes asked him how dared he take so long, leave him sitting in this new bed that he wasn't sure how to get out of?

'This isn't how it's supposed to be, Harry,' Dominic said, because surely it should be a sweet, cherubic baby sitting there smiling at him, but it was an angry Harry with a full nappy. The newly engaged Dominic had to change the first nappy in his life and, yes, it was shocking, a real baptism of fire!

'Think of all the cruises I won't be going on,' Dominic said as he tried to work out all the tabs, 'all the sheer irresponsibility I'm missing...'

'Hey!' Harry said, liking his clean bottom and new word.

'Hey,' Dominic answered

And then he picked him up.

A bare chest, a toddler who was still a baby and a mass of curls against his chin, and it *was* inevitable— he didn't just love Bridgette, he loved Harry too. For the second time in twenty minutes he handed over his heart and it was terrifying.

He would never tell, but he thought he was crying. Maybe he was because Harry's fat hands were patting his cheeks. He could never tell Bridgette that he was terrified too.

That the phone might ring.

That there might be a knock on the door.

That Courtney might come back.

That this little guy might have to be returned too soon.

'I'll make this work.' He looked into the little grey eyes that had always been wary and saw the trust in them now. 'I will make this work,' Dominic said again, and his commitment was as solid as the diamond he had placed on Bridgette's finger—his promise to Harry would cut glass if it had to, it was that strong. 'It will all be okay.'

He walked back into the bedroom with a sweet-smelling Harry and did a double-take as he saw his previously sexy fiancée in bright orange flannelette pyjama bottoms and a T-shirt.

'Don't want him having flashbacks about his aunt in years to come,' Bridgette said.

And it was hard, because she was more a mother than the one Harry had.

'I'm just going to wash my hands.'

He was so tidy and neat. As he handed over Harry and headed to the bedroom, she worked something out. 'That's why he smiled,' Bridgette said. 'When you took your jacket off, he knew that you were staying.'

She looked at her nephew, at smiling grey eyes that mirrored her own, and it was easy to say it as Dominic walked back in the room.

'I love you.'

EPILOGUE

BRIDGETTE never got tired of watching a new life come into the world. It had been a glorious morning and had been a wonderful straightforward birth. Kate was watching from the bed, and Michael, the father, was standing over Bridgette as she finished up the weights and measurements, popped on a hat, wrapped up their son and handed him over—the perfect miracle, really.

'We're going to move you back to your room soon,' Bridgette told the new parents. 'I'll come and check on you later, but Jasmine is going to take over from me for a little while.'

'That's right.' Kate looked up from her baby. 'You've got your scan this morning. I'm glad he arrived in time and you didn't have to dash off.'

'I wouldn't have left you,' Bridgette said. 'I'd already rung down and told them I might not be able to leave.' She looked at the little pink squashed face and smiled. 'You have a very considerate baby.'

'You'll have one of your own soon.'

'Not that soon.' Bridgette gave an impatient sigh, because she really couldn't wait. 'I'm only nineteen weeks.' And then she checked herself, because she sounded just like any impatient first-time mum, and then she laughed because that was exactly what she was. She gave a small wink. 'Nineteen weeks and counting!'

She would breathe when she got to twenty-four weeks, she decided, no, twenty-five, she corrected, thinking of the difference those extra few days had made to Francesca. Francesca had been discharged the day Dominic had started his new job—home on oxygen but doing brilliantly. It had been a nice way to start, Dominic had said.

As she walked down to the canteen where she was meeting Dominic, she wondered if he'd be able to get away. She really didn't mind if he couldn't. It was a routine scan, after all, and he'd end up asking the sonographer way too many questions. Still, even if she would be fine without him, she smiled when she saw him sitting at the far end of the canteen, sharing lunch with Harry, and she realised he was going to make the appointment—it was better with him there.

'Hi, Harry.' She received a lovely kiss that tasted of bananas, and asked about his busy morning, because along with building bricks he'd done a painting or two, or was it three? He really had come on in leaps and bounds. 'Any news from Courtney?' Bridgette asked Dominic.

'I was about to ask you the same,' Dominic said. 'She seems to be taking ages. I thought it started at eleven.'

Courtney had an interview this morning at the hospital. She was attending college, and now that she had been clean for well over a year, she was applying for a job on the drug and alcohol unit. But as much as Bridgette wanted her sister to get the job and to do well, she was a little bit torn, not quite sure that Courtney was ready for such a demanding role. Courtney lived in Bridgette's old flat, paid a minimal rent and had been working hard in every area of her life. Although Bridgette was unsure about this job, she was also worried how Courtney would take it if she was turned down when she had such high hopes.

'We're about to find out,' Dominic said, and she looked up as Courtney made her way over.

'How did you go?' Bridgette asked.

'I didn't get it,' Courtney said, which seemed contrary to her smile as she kissed her little boy. 'They don't think I'm quite ready to work with addicts yet. I need more time sorting out myself and they said that there was another course I should think about, but—' she gave a very wide smile '—they were very impressed with me. Apparently there is a position as a domestic. The patients do a lot of the cleaning work, but I would be in charge of the kitchen, sort of overseeing things.' She pulled a face. 'And I have to do the toilets and bathrooms. It's three days a week for now and some weekends, but they'll also pay me to do the course.' She gave a nervous swallow. 'Really, it's like a full-time job.'

'Oh, my!' Bridgette beamed. 'It sounds perfect.' Then laughed. 'Except I can't really imagine you keeping things clean.'

'She's such a bossy landlady, isn't she, Harry?'

Courtney said, and Bridgette admitted that, yes, maybe at times she was. 'I have to go to the uniform room and then down to HR. I'd better get him back.'

'We'll take Harry back to daycare,' Dominic said, rather than offered, because Harry was still eating. 'That way he can finish his lunch.'

He was very firm with Courtney, didn't play games with her, didn't bend to any to her whims, and he didn't let Bridgette bend too far either.

Courtney breezed off and Dominic rolled his eyes. 'She's doing great and everything, but she's still the most self-absorbed person that I've ever met.' He let out a wry laugh. 'She didn't even wish you luck for your scan.'

'That's Courtney.'

With Harry's lunch finished, they headed back to daycare but at the last minute, as he handed Harry over to Mary, it was Dominic who changed his mind. 'Should we bring him?'

'To the ultrasound?' Bridgette frowned at Mary. 'Won't it upset him?'

'It might be a wonderful way to get him used to the idea,' Mary said. 'After all he's going to be like a big brother.'

'I guess,' Bridgette said, because Harry was going to be a brother to this baby, even if not in the conventional way... And that just about summed them up entirely. It was as if Harry had three parents. Even if Courtney was doing brilliantly, it hadn't been the smoothest of rides, and it was an ongoing journey. As Dominic had once pointed out, Harry deserved the extra ration of love and he got it, over and over—from his mum, from his aunt and her husband, from his grandparents too, who made a far more regular fuss of him.

So as Dominic held Harry, Bridgette lay on the bed and the ultrasound started. 'Are we going to find out?' She still couldn't decide if she wanted to know the sex or wanted the surprise.

'I am,' Dominic said, studying the screen closely, and she felt sorry for the sonographer with this brusque paediatrician in the room. 'Don't worry, I won't let on.' He wouldn't; Bridgette knew that much. He was the best in the world at keeping it all in. It had taken ages to work him out and she was still doing it, would be doing it for the rest of her life no doubt—but it was the most pleasurable job in the world.

She heard the clicks and the measurements being taken and felt the probe moving over her stomach. She looked over to where Dominic and Harry were closely observing the screen and then she laughed because there *he* was doing somersaults, a little cousin for Harry, and a nephew for Chris, who would be the most devoted uncle in the world.

'Everything looks normal.' The sonographer smiled and then she spoke to Dominic. 'Did you want to have a look?'

She saw him hover, could almost hear the ten million questions whizzing around that brilliant brain, knew he wanted to take the probe and check and check again that everything was perfect, that everything was just so, but with supreme effort Dominic gave a small shake of his head.

'"Normal" sounds pretty good,' he said, 'and it's not as if we'll be sending it back.'

Already their family was perfect.

* * * * *

Mills & Boon® Hardback
June 2012

ROMANCE

A Secret Disgrace	Penny Jordan
The Dark Side of Desire	Julia James
The Forbidden Ferrara	Sarah Morgan
The Truth Behind his Touch	Cathy Williams
Enemies at the Altar	Melanie Milburne
A World She Doesn't Belong To	Natasha Tate
In Defiance of Duty	Caitlin Crews
In the Italian's Sights	Helen Brooks
Dare She Kiss & Tell?	Aimee Carson
Waking Up In The Wrong Bed	Natalie Anderson
Plain Jane in the Spotlight	Lucy Gordon
Battle for the Soldier's Heart	Cara Colter
It Started with a Crush...	Melissa McClone
The Navy Seal's Bride	Soraya Lane
My Greek Island Fling	Nina Harrington
A Girl Less Ordinary	Leah Ashton
Sydney Harbour Hospital: Bella's Wishlist	Emily Forbes
Celebrity in Braxton Falls	Judy Campbell

HISTORICAL

The Duchess Hunt	Elizabeth Beacon
Marriage of Mercy	Carla Kelly
Chained to the Barbarian	Carol Townend
My Fair Concubine	Jeannie Lin

MEDICAL

Doctor's Mile-High Fling	Tina Beckett
Hers For One Night Only?	Carol Marinelli
Unlocking the Surgeon's Heart	Jessica Matthews
Marriage Miracle in Swallowbrook	Abigail Gordon

Mills & Boon® Large Print
June 2012

ROMANCE

An Offer She Can't Refuse	Emma Darcy
An Indecent Proposition	Carol Marinelli
A Night of Living Dangerously	Jennie Lucas
A Devilishly Dark Deal	Maggie Cox
The Cop, the Puppy and Me	Cara Colter
Back in the Soldier's Arms	Soraya Lane
Miss Prim and the Billionaire	Lucy Gordon
Dancing with Danger	Fiona Harper

HISTORICAL

The Disappearing Duchess	Anne Herries
Improper Miss Darling	Gail Whitiker
Beauty and the Scarred Hero	Emily May
Butterfly Swords	Jeannie Lin

MEDICAL

New Doc in Town	Meredith Webber
Orphan Under the Christmas Tree	Meredith Webber
The Night Before Christmas	Alison Roberts
Once a Good Girl...	Wendy S. Marcus
Surgeon in a Wedding Dress	Sue MacKay
The Boy Who Made Them Love Again	Scarlet Wilson

Mills & Boon® Hardback

July 2012

ROMANCE

MEDICAL

Mills & Boon® Large Print

July 2012

ROMANCE

Roccanti's Marriage Revenge	Lynne Graham
The Devil and Miss Jones	Kate Walker
Sheikh Without a Heart	Sandra Marton
Savas's Wildcat	Anne McAllister
A Bride for the Island Prince	Rebecca Winters
The Nanny and the Boss's Twins	Barbara McMahon
Once a Cowboy...	Patricia Thayer
When Chocolate Is Not Enough...	Nina Harrington

HISTORICAL

The Mysterious Lord Marlowe	Anne Herries
Marrying the Royal Marine	Carla Kelly
A Most Unladylike Adventure	Elizabeth Beacon
Seduced by Her Highland Warrior	Michelle Willingham

MEDICAL

The Boss She Can't Resist	Lucy Clark
Heart Surgeon, Hero...Husband?	Susan Carlisle
Dr Langley: Protector or Playboy?	Joanna Neil
Daredevil and Dr Kate	Leah Martyn
Spring Proposal in Swallowbrook	Abigail Gordon
Doctor's Guide to Dating in the Jungle	Tina Beckett

0612 GEN STD LP